G000037449

K. SEAN HARRIS

For Lawrence

THE
KINGDOM OF DEATH

*Will Terri survive her latest battle as she
attempts to bring a powerful murderer to justice?*

Sean

23.08. ₵2

Cover concept by: K. Sean Harris
Cover Design by: Sanya Dockery
Book Design, Layout & Typesetting by: Sanya Dockery

Published by: Book Fetish

Printed in the U.S.A.   ISBN: 978-976-95303-4-8

NATIONAL LIBRARY OF JAMAICA CATALOGUING-IN-PUBLICATION DATA

Harris, K. Sean
        The kingdom of death / by K. Sean Harris

        p. ; cm.
ISBN 978-976-95303-4-8 (pbk)

1. Jamaican fiction
I. Title

813   dc 22

Then when lust hath conceived, it bringeth forth sin: and sin, when it is finished, bringeth forth death.

JAMES 1: 15

For a whore is a deep ditch; and a strange woman is a narrow pit.

PROVERBS 23: 27

ALSO BY K. SEAN HARRIS:

Novels

Queen of the Damned

Blood of Angels

Kiss of Death

The Garrison

The Heart Collector

Death Incarnate

The Stud

The Stud 11

Merchants of Death

Anthologies

The Sex Files

The Sex Files Vol. 2

Erotic Jamaican Tales

More Erotic Jamaican Tales

PROLOGUE

Cocaine. The devil's dandruff. He sniffed the entire eight-inch long line through his right nostril, a solitary manicured finger pressed against the left, as the addictive white powder noisily disappeared from off the top of the glass and mahogany table. He then raised his head, the cocaine residue on his bulbous nose a stark contrast to his extremely dark face, and smiled lustfully at the beautiful naked woman sitting spread-eagled, as instructed, on the red leather loveseat.

She returned his smile, masking her hatred well. She despised him but she had no choice. He was a member of The Circle; a small, secret, tightly-knit alliance of powerful politicians and businessmen. She had met one of them six months ago and though she had received numerous gifts and her bank account had swollen significantly in that period, she was not happy. The man had introduced her to the rest of The Circle and since then, she was constantly in demand by all ten of them. Some of them were very vile creatures, requiring the most sadistic sexual acts. It was taking a toll on her. She wanted out, and had said as much a month ago to the one whom she first met. The look he gave her had chilled her soul. He told her that the only way she would be free of them was when they got tired of her, which wouldn't be any time soon.

They spoke freely in front of her as well, with no fear that a call girl, no doubt in awe of their wealth and considerable power, would dare breathe a word of anything she heard to anyone, discussing sensitive matters which if disclosed, would cause ripples at the highest levels of Jamaican society. It unnerved her to no end. She had to get out. She was stressed and increasingly afraid. They had started paying her less and less for her services. A query the first time it happened, had resulted in all ten having their way with her in a 24 hour period, for free.

She wanted to flee the country but they had eyes everywhere. They would know. She was a prisoner, trapped in their powerful web.

She sighed inwardly as the man approached her, the cocaine making him walk like he was floating on air. She was in for a rough night. This one was very virile and well endowed, and when he was high off cocaine, which was usually the case, he sometimes lasted for hours on end. It was as though the cocaine went directly to his genitals and she suspected that he was also using Viagra or a similar product. Though he was in great shape, a man his age could not naturally possess so much stamina. She prayed that he paid her tonight.

He reached her and roughly gripped a fistful of her silky mane. She tried not to grimace, forcing the smile to stay on her face as she moved her head downwards, complying with his nonverbal request. He tightened his grip, growling like a rabid dog as she pleasured him.

She couldn't wait for the night to be over.

CHAPTER 1

The tinted white sport utility vehicle turned onto West King's House Road and pulled over a few meters pass a gated apartment complex. Though this was an upper middleclass neighbourhood in Kingston, it was an area frequented by prostitutes, and was a well used thoroughfare by motorists as it allowed them to cut out some of the traffic if they were heading uptown. But the streets were deserted tonight; at least the occupants of the vehicle didn't see anyone around.

The left rear door swung open and the partially nude, dead body of a young woman was unceremoniously thrown from the back seat. The body landed on the sidewalk facedown with a loud thud, the head cocked at a slightly awkward angle. A white Hermés pocketbook followed, hitting her back before settling down on the cold concrete beside its owner. Her once beautiful face was battered almost beyond recognition. Her eyes were wide open. They silently spoke of unimaginable horrors. She had not died an easy death.

The door slammed shut and the vehicle drove off, heading uptown. A woman cautiously stepped out of the shadows on the opposite side of the road, and crossed the street. She was thankful that she had followed her instincts and did not go out into the light when she had seen the headlights of the approaching vehicle. Her instincts never failed. They had saved her the night when she declined to go into a car with a man who just didn't seem right to her, despite the fact that he was offering her twice the usual amount. A girl further down the street had gone with him and her body was found in a ditch the following morning, about fifty miles from where the man had picked her up. She held down her short dress as the wind – uncommonly strong due to a surface level trough in the central Caribbean which was influencing the weather in Jamaica – threatened to lift it, exposing her uncovered private parts.

She looked at the dead woman with desensitized eyes. It wasn't the first dead body she was seeing and it wouldn't be the last. She decided to go home. Pretty soon, once the body was discovered, the police would cordon the entire area and she didn't want to get caught up in that. Witnesses didn't fare well in Jamaica and besides, what had she seen? Nothing of consequence, though she knew the make and colour of the vehicle. She quickly searched the small pocketbook, extracting a wad of cash. She would have taken the pocketbook but the plush white leather was decorated with blood. She stuffed the money in her bosom and walked away hurriedly, turning up the street and heading out on to Hope Road. She would go to Half-Way-Tree, buy some jerk chicken and take a cab home. It had been a slow, windy night but she was lucky. She didn't know how much money she had gotten from the purse but it was definitely more than she had made all night.

She checked the time.

It was 3 a.m.

She wondered if her boyfriend was home.

CHAPTER 2

Martin Meyers was in his bedroom, sitting up in his king-sized bed with a tray, having breakfast and watching the 64 inch Plasma T.V. on the wall when he saw the news report. He chewed his egg and cheese sandwich slowly as he paid rapt attention. The body of a dead woman had been found on West King's House Road early that morning. Police theorize that she had been killed elsewhere and her body dumped where it was found. Her driver's license was on the screen as the news reporter asked anyone who knew her to contact the police.

Meyers sipped his coffee thoughtfully. Alexandra Fletcher was dead. Murdered. He remembered the day the beautiful, demure, twenty-four year old woman had come to see him at his office. He had just gotten in when his secretary, the dependable Mrs. Roper, buzzed him that there was a young woman here to see him without an appointment. To this day he didn't know what had prompted him to see her. He didn't accept walk-ins and he had a very busy day ahead, yet he had seen her.

He was shocked when she entered his office. He hadn't expected her to be so young and beautiful. It was the strangest meeting he had ever had.

"Good morning, Mr. Meyers," she said, extending a small, manicured hand. "I'm Alexandra Fletcher."

"Good morning, Ms. Fletcher," he replied, drinking in her startling natural beauty as he shook her hand, holding it longer than necessary.

"Thank you for seeing me." *Her large, doe-like brown eyes looked sad and frightened.*

"No problem," he lied. He was due in court in three hours and needed to go over some notes. "How can I help you?"

"I would like you to keep a parcel for me – it's nothing illegal – and in the event of my demise, turn it over to Superintendent of Police Terri Miller, no one else."

Meyers looked at her, his brain churning. There were a million questions he wanted to ask, but wasn't sure which one he wanted to ask first.

"Please don't ask me to go into details," she continued, "because I can't. Will you do this for me and if so, how much will it cost?"

Meyers looked at her for what seemed like an eternity. Either this woman was a nutcase – and he didn't think that was the case – or her life was really in danger. Why wasn't she doing something about this apparent threat to her life instead of resigning herself to her fate and hoping the perpetrator gets punished by whatever evidence she was leaving in the package? But he couldn't ask, and she wouldn't tell. Either he would help, or he wouldn't, that's all she wanted to know.

He decided he would. There was something about her that tugged at his heart strings. He would help her. Hopefully he would never have to give Terri Miller that package.

"Ok, this is very unorthodox but I'll help you," he told her.

"Thank you so much," she said, smiling a weak but grateful smile. "How much?"

Meyers thought for awhile. How much should he charge her for something like this? He decided to only charge her for the visit, treat it as a consultancy.

"Ten thousand dollars," he replied.

She nodded and removed the package from her baby blue, gold studded Prada handbag. It was a small bubble envelope, addressed to Superintendent of Police Terri Miller. He took it from her and told her to pay Mrs. Roper when she went back out to the reception area and collect her receipt.

She stood and extended her hand.

"*Thanks again,*" *she told him.* "*I really appreciate this.*"

Meyers didn't want her to go. She intrigued him. He wanted to get to know the mysterious and beautiful young woman. But he knew that wasn't going to happen.

"*My pleasure,*" *he said simply, knowing he would never see her again.*

They shook hands and she left his office, leaving behind a faint but alluring whiff of Leau Dissey by Issey Miyake.

Feeling unsettled and very curious, he googled her name and nearly went into cardiac arrest when he saw her personal web page.

She was a prostitute. Or a courtesan as she put it. His head spun. There were six pictures of her in various modes of dress. There were two swimsuit shots, two in spectacular evening gowns, and two in lingerie. She looked absolutely stunning. She had a virgin/whore complex thing going on, her beautiful innocent face be-lying her profession. There was only an email address for contact information and there were no prices. 'If you have to ask, you can't afford me' she proclaimed. Wow. He was seeing it but he couldn't believe it. He didn't know what he thought that the beautiful, obvi-ously well-bred young woman did for a living, but he never in a million years would've guessed this.

He minimized her page and went back to the search results. She was featured on the web site for an upper class Gentlemen's Club in Las Vegas as a host. He clicked on her picture. 'No longer an employee' was the result. Strange that they would still have her picture up. He could only surmise that they kept it on there for the eye candy. The other five women featured were hot but she stood out.

He leaned back in his chair, processing this remarkable discovery. He decided to contact her. He went back to her page and sent her an email. The message bounced. The email address was no longer valid. He sighed. It was a long time before he was able to get his work day going. She had completely turned his morning upside down.

That had been a month ago, and now she was dead. He would contact Terri Miller as soon as he got to the office. He hoped that the contents of the package would indeed lead to her killers. The poor girl did not deserve to have her life cut so short. He buzzed his helper on the kitchen intercom to come and collect his tray.

He had lost his appetite.

CHAPTER 3

Terri Miller pulled up in her reserved parking spot at Police Headquarters at 9 a.m. She had just dropped off her six year old son, Marc-Anthony, at the ultra-exclusive preparatory school that he attended. The school was only available to the children of diplomats, powerful politicians, prominent businessmen, and celebrity parents of a certain stature. Terri was deathly afraid of someone kidnapping Marc-Anthony to get to her, so the well-secured private school was a godsend. It had been five years since the sensational *Wolf Man* case and though it had almost claimed her life, the spin off from the international publicity the case had generated was nothing short of incredible. She had been a guest on the Oprah Winfrey Show as well as the David Letterman Show, and she made a guest appearance on CSI: Miami as a clinical psychologist.

She had also received the keys to the city from Kingston's mayor, was bestowed the Medal of Gallantry by the Jamaican Government and she was the most recognizable female face in Jamaica.

She had not had a case as dangerous to deal with since and she thanked God for that. She hoped fervently that it remained that way. She had been able to spend a lot of quality time with her son over the past few years and that meant the world to her. He was a very precocious child, way smarter than she had been at his age, and that was saying a lot. She grabbed her pocketbook, exited her recently purchased SUV, a white Mercedes ML320, and made her way inside Jamaica Towers, the tallest building in the island. She rode the elevator up to the twelfth floor where her office was located.

Mrs. Green, her secretary, bade her a hearty good morning and went to fetch her coffee. Terri went inside her office and closed the door. She removed her blazer and hung it in the small closet that was next to her private bathroom. She then settled down at her desk and went through the pile of messages that Mrs. Green had left for her. By the time she had dealt with the first two, Mrs. Green knocked softly on the door and came in with a steaming mug of Blue Mountain coffee. She placed it on the large, neatly-kept mahogany desk and quietly left without saying a word.

Terri took a sip as she looked at the third message. It was from Martin Meyers, an attorney, and it was urgent. He had called twice this morning. She wondered what that was about. She used her cordless phone to return his call as she swiveled her chair to face the large glass window behind her. She looked down at the bustling Thursday morning traffic as a woman answered the phone and told her to hold. Four seconds later, Martin Meyers was on the line.

"Good morning Superintendent Miller," he said, sounding anxious or nervous, Terri wasn't sure which. "Thank you for getting back to me so quickly."

"Good morning, Mr. Meyers," Terri responded. "Not a problem. How can I help you?"

"I have a sensitive matter that I need to discuss with you in person," he told her.

Terri didn't respond immediately.

"I know that's not saying much but it's really something that I don't want to get into over the phone," he pressed. "It is relevant to a murder that took place recently."

"I see," Terri responded finally, quickly scanning her diary to see when she could meet with him. "Come and see me at headquarters promptly at 12:30."

"Ok, thank you," he said. "See you then."

Terri terminated the call and looked out the window thoughtfully. She wondered which recent murder he

11

was referring to. There had been several. Sad to say but someone got murdered almost every day. It saddened her to no end the way her people had become so bloodthirsty. Even the kids had joined in on the act. Just yesterday, a tenth grader had been stabbed a mere three inches from his heart by another student that attended the same high school. And it wasn't just Jamaica. So many crazy things were happening all over the world. The other day, a teenager had shot and killed nine students and three teachers at his former high school in Germany, before being killed by police. Terri ruefully wondered if the Mayan Prophecy was right and the world would indeed come to an end on December 21, 2012.

<hr />

Mrs. Roper, Martin Meyers' secretary, after listening in on the call that her boss just had with the esteemed Superintendent, used her cell phone to make a call to someone whom she only knew as *Understanding*. She had received a visit in the parking lot a month ago when she was about to head home after work. A well dressed man, in full black and wearing over sized sunglasses, had approached her with a proposition. Do what he asked, and be paid for her time, or face danger. She realized that it was not an idle threat when he quietly told her where she lived, who she lived with and the name and address of the young man with whom she was having an affair.

In a daze, she had answered all of the man's questions as best she could and followed his instructions. He wanted to know why the young woman, Alexandra Fletcher, had come by the office to meet with Martin Meyers. She had not learnt the reason for the young woman's visit and her casual conversation about the woman to Meyers had yielded nothing. The man had instructed her to monitor Meyers' calls and visitors closely, and report to him anything of interest. She had gone to the ATM machine on the same plaza where her favourite supermarket was located a week after meeting the man, and after making a withdrawal, she noticed that her balance was fifty thousand dollars more. She felt guilty about spying on Meyers. He was a good boss, very kind and easy to work for. But she had to do what she had to do. These people, whoever they were, scared her to death. She would do whatever they asked.

"About time you did something useful," the man who called himself *Understanding* said after she told him about the call.

He hung up and lit his cigar, a Cuban import that he was hopelessly addicted to, and looked at the small flat screen TV on the wall. It was on CNN and there was breaking news about the attack on the Sri Lankan cricket team by militants. He thought about the information that he had just received. The lawyer was going to see Terri Miller regarding a recent murder. Alexandra Fletcher had gone to see him a little over a month ago. She was recently killed. He didn't believe in coincidences. The lawyer was going to see Terri Miller about Fletcher.

What exactly did he know? *Understanding* blew out perfect smoke rings. His intense eyes crinkled with pleasure. It wasn't easy to create perfect Os and he had mastered the art. He wasn't overly concerned. Terri Miller getting involved was an unexpected development in a matter that The Circle had basically considered closed – who cared about a dead whore? – but it was nothing that they couldn't handle. Martin Meyers would be apprehended after his meeting with the Superintendent. They would learn what he knew and take it from there.

He would interrogate him personally.

CHAPTER 4

Martin Meyers entered Terri Miller's expansive office wearing a grey suit with a pink paisley tie and a nervous smile. He had arrived ten minutes early for his appointment and was shown in at exactly 12:30 by Mrs. Green, who with her quiet efficiency and pleasant but no-nonsense demeanour, reminded him of his secretary, Mrs. Roper.

Terri rose to meet him.

"Good afternoon, Superintendent Miller," he said, surprised at her very firm, almost masculine handshake.

"Good morning, Mr. Meyers. Have a seat."

Meyers sat down on one of the three leather chairs in front of her desk.

She clasped her elegant, well-manicured hands on her lap and looked at him, waiting for him to begin. Meyers had seen her on countless occasions but never in person. She was a very beautiful woman. Flawless, creamy skin; large, inviting light brown eyes; pouty, soft-looking lips; small aristocratic nose and long, beautiful hair which was currently in a tight bun, emphasizing her prominent cheekbones.

It was difficult not to stare.

He cleared his throat and told her about the strange visit to his office by the murdered prostitute a little over a month ago. He also related to her what he had seen on the internet. Terri listened attentively, without interrupting.

Meyers reached into his cowhide leather attaché case and retrieved the small package. He handed it to her. She took it and placed it on the desk.

"Thank you very much for coming to see me," she told him, rising to shake his hand, indicating that the meeting was over. "I'll be in touch if necessary."

Meyers rose slowly, a bit disappointed. He wasn't sure what he had expected but he had expected something more. She hadn't even commented on the information that he gave her.

"My pleasure," he replied.

He then took his leave and closed the door softly behind him.

Terri then buzzed Mrs. Green and instructed her that she was not to be disturbed for the next hour.

She took up the package, a small bubble envelope, and used a pair of scissors to open it.

Ok, let's see what we have here.

She removed the contents of the envelope. It was a small address book. Her eyebrows arched in surprise as she went through the book page by page. She recognized a few of the names. Alexandra Fletcher's clientele was upper class. There was a powerful politician, a head of a corporation, and a prominent businessman.

Terri frowned at some of the names. They were very unusual: *Knowledge, Wisdom, Understanding, Culture, Power, Equality, God, Build, Born* and *Cipher*. They all had a circle next to them. Instinctively, she knew that these names were very important. What did they mean? Who were the people that these names represented? What was the significance of the circle? Terri got up and went over to the small photo copy machine to the right of her desk. She copied all forty two pages of the small book and placed the copies inside her pocketbook. She would lock them in her safe at home. She went over to the window and looked down at the bustling metropolis that was New Kingston.

Someone very important had killed Alexandra Fletcher.

Someone in that book.

Why?

Who?

She had obviously expected something to happen

to her. So why hadn't she explicitly identified the source of the threat to her life? Why did she only leave her address book? She had wanted Terri to have the book. Perhaps she thought that only Terri could figure it out and bring her murderer to justice.

Terri could feel the adrenaline flowing.

The case intrigued her.

She was going to make it her priority.

stop

4/07/02

10 a.m

CHAPTER 5

"Excuse me, sir," a deep, gravelly voice said to Martin Meyers as he opened the door to his silver BMW sedan. He turned around and his body shook comically as a man, holding a taser while advancing towards him, sent electrical currents into his one hundred and ninety pound frame. The taser, a X26 model favoured by law enforcement officers in the United States, was effective from as far as thirty-six feet away. At five feet away it was almost lethal. The man held Meyers' slumping, almost unconscious frame, and placed him in a black Mitsubishi Pajero which was parked next to Meyers' car. The SUV then exited the parking lot with measured haste, followed by Meyers' car which was being driven by a member of the four-man kidnapping team.

A woman, a forty-nine year old widow who was supposed to be meeting with a senior detective regarding an embezzlement case, was shocked at what she had just witnessed. Parked directly across from where the incident occurred, she was about to exit her car when she realized what was happening. Shaking despite the sweltering early afternoon heat, she hurriedly went inside Police Headquarters. She was scared but considered it her civic duty to report what she had just seen. She would tell the same cop that she would be meeting with shortly.

⁂

Martin Meyers was scared. He had never been more afraid in his entire life. He struggled to remain calm. He was kidnapped. Plucked away from his car like it was nothing, on the premises of Police Headquarters no less. He was in the back of a tinted SUV, sandwiched between two men. They had yet to say a word to him. He wanted to ask a million questions but doubted he would receive an answer. They might even tase him again. Best to remain quiet until they voiced their intentions. He was no longer dazed. Apparently there were no long term effects from being tasered. He considered himself lucky though. People have been known to die after being tasered. Only fear remained. What was this about? What were they going to do to him?

The host of a popular day time radio talk show was arguing with a caller about what were the main reasons for the rise in crime. They were now in Manor Park. They drove pass his favourite plaza to shop for work attire and headed on to Norbrook Drive. His heart raced. For a moment he thought that they were heading to his home but they passed his street and turned left onto Hill Run Road. His mother, who was suffering from Alzheimer's, and the nurse who helped to take care of her, were at his home and he wouldn't want any harm to come to them. They stopped at the black wrought iron gate of a huge off-white, Spanish styled mansion. The massive electronic gate swung open and they entered the premises, drove up the cobblestone driveway, and then pulled into an enclosed garage.

Why hadn't they blindfolded him? He could easily identify these men in an identification parade and finding this house would be a breeze. Then it hit him. They hadn't bothered to hide anything because they were going to kill him. He would never leave this place alive.

He panicked.

CHAPTER 6

Detective Corporal Foster listened with a frown as Ms. Braithwaite, who suspected her lawyer of fleecing her money, related what she had seen in the parking lot. He made notes as she gave him a detailed account. Interesting. And alarming. He would bring it to Superintendent Miller's attention. They then moved on to discussing her fears that there were some irregularities in the business transactions and investments that her lawyer had been conducting on her behalf. The woman was right. The lawyer, cleverly at first but getting bolder and sloppier as he encountered success, was robbing her blind. Ms. Braithwaite was a wealthy, relatively young widow and the lawyer had been representing the family for over ten years. He had started swindling the woman's money six months after the husband passed away two years ago. She had finally caught up with him. And now, so had the law. Foster assured the woman that they would put all the evidence together, and within a week, he would be arrested. She thanked him and left with him in tow. She had asked him to escort her to her car, and he had kindly agreed, knowing that she was still shaken by the kidnapping that she had witnessed.

꧁ᘛⵣᘚ꧂

After a delicious lunch of roasted tender baby pork glazed with honey, sautéed potatoes and fettuccine with tomato and basil at The Boiler Room, an exclusive Kingston eatery, Terri made her way over to Barbican, where Alexandra Fletcher had resided in a one bed-room apartment. The detective on the case – who was relieved of it by Terri via a memo she had sent to him – had turned over the thin file that he had amassed since the discovery of the woman's body. The house had already been visited by a team of detectives but according to the file, nothing of consequence had been found. She hummed along to the Jennifer Hudson single *If This Isn't Love* as she headed across the busy intersection.

She thought of Nico. Nico Sanchez. It had taken another Latino to break her out of her self imposed relationship exile. He was the first man since Anthony to break through the barrier she had constructed after

Anthony's death. She had met him a year after the *Wolf Man* case while on a weekend shopping excursion in New York. She had just exited the revamped Dolce & Gabbana flag ship store on Madison Avenue when she bumped into his six foot tall wiry frame draped in a blue and white cardigan, v-neck white T and fitted jeans. He had looked down on his scuffed Pirelli loafers ruefully.

"Don't you just hate when that happens?" he had said, transferring his gaze from his loafers to her flushed face.

"I'm so sorry," Terri had replied, wondering what was happening to her. She was feeling something that she hadn't felt in a long time. Five years to be exact. Interest. It was the first time since Anthony that she had felt that towards any man. It had startled her. Caught her off guard. It was a bit frightening yet exciting at the same time.

"I accept your apology," he smiled, adding, "but only on one condition..."

Terri returned his smile, trying to ignore the butterflies in her stomach.

"And what might that be?" she asked.

He took her free hand.

His touch made her gasp. It was like he had electrocuted her. This was no joke. It almost felt like the first time she met Anthony.

Almost.

"If you agree to have lunch with me," he said, tucking her arm into his and turning up the street with her.

"This is kidnapping, Mr. I-don't-even-know-your-name," Terri protested, though she didn't resist. She wondered if he could hear how loudly her heart was beating.

"Call the police," he had responded.

"I am the police."

He had chuckled at that as they slowly made their way up the bustling street, arm in arm like new lovers as opposed to total strangers.

"Which precinct?" he asked.

"The Jamaica Police Force," she replied.

"Hmm...seems like you are out of your jurisdiction, Mrs. Officer," he teased.

Terri chuckled wryly.

"I guess I am," she admitted.

They had lunched at Andre's Café, a Hungarian eatery on the Upper East Side. Terri guiltily enjoyed a calorie laden lunch of Hungarian country platter which consisted of Hungarian salami, sausage, bacon and cheese, with red onion and green pepper, served with bread and butter, while Nico had Korozott in Paprika consisting of feta and cream cheese blended with onion, paprika and spices with tomato and bread.

Lunch lasted for two hours but they had barely noticed. They had chatted comfortably, as though they had known each other for quite some time. Nico was fascinated by the fact that she had been the Jamaican cop involved in that horrible *Wolf Man* case a few years ago. He was very impressed at what she had accomplished in her career in only nine years. When Terri had finally gotten him to talk about himself, she learnt that he was a successful sports agent whose clientele boasted a star NFL running back, a rising NBA point guard and a veteran NBA small forward who had won a championship with the Boston Celtics in 2008. He also dabbled in music, and had bankrolled an album for an indie artist who fused jazz, hip hop and R&B in her music. The album had quietly sold six hundred thousand copies worldwide – not bad for an independent release by an underground artist – and he had profited considerably on his investment.

He was with her every available moment for the rest of the weekend. They had dinner together that night, after which he took her to a Broadway play and on the Sunday, her final day as she was flying on the late flight out to Jamaica that night, they watched a Knicks game at Madison Square Garden. It had been a wonderful weekend. The temptation to sleep with him was great but she had managed to resist. They had kept in touch over the course of the next few months and became quite close, due to their long telephone conversations and constant emails whenever time permitted.

She finally caved in four months after that enjoyable weekend and they met in Puerto Rico, where his father was from, for a weekend that had taken her breath away. They had stayed at an all-inclusive hotel in Coco Beach, located at the eastern end of the island. She had ended her drought in fine style. He couldn't replace Anthony in her heart – she didn't think anyone could – but she was in love with him. He was exciting, intelligent, funny, hot, fashionable and excellent in bed. Very impressive resume.

It was not easy maintaining a long distance relationship and she had yet to introduce him to her son – which she was dreading – but so far so good. The next time they were going to see each other he would be coming to Jamaica. She was nervously excited about his pending visit. They would have to be low key. She didn't want the press all up in her love life.

Terri arrived at Salisbury Place, where the young woman had lived, and the security guard let her into the complex quickly after she showed him her ID. The landlord, as instructed, had left a key to the apartment with the guard.

Terri frowned when she entered the apartment. The place was ransacked. The cops who had visited the apartment had done a thorough search, though Terri was sure that they didn't have a clue what they were looking for. She stepped over a sofa cushion and went into the bedroom. Clothing spilled out of half open drawers and the mattress was halfway on the floor, leaning up against the bed. Terri looked at the clothing. Expensive stuff. So were her perfumes, make-up and body crèmes. This had been a woman who took care of herself. Terri ventured into the bathroom and looked inside the medicine cabinet. Sleeping pills. Headache medicine. Pills for anal pain.

Somebody was having problems sleeping and was very stressed out, Terri mused as she ventured out to the kitchen. *Somebody's rectum had also been tampered with.*

Nothing that she saw in the medicine cabinet surprised her. The woman, knowing that there was a threat on her life, had understandably been stressed and had problems sleeping, and the medicine for anal pain was probably due to too much strenuous activity back there.

Alexandra Fletcher had been a healthy eater. Oats, cans of salmon, low fat milk, and granola cereal, lined the kitchen cupboards while the refrigerator was filled with fruits, eggs, vegetables, fruit juice and water.

Terri went back out to the living room. She noticed a small computer desk. It was empty. She made a note to check with the detective that had been handling the case. She did not recall there being a computer on the small list of items that they took from the woman's home. After a few more minutes, Terri left. She was thoughtful as she made her way to her SUV. There had been nothing personal in the apartment with the exception of the woman's clothes and toiletries. No photographs of Fletcher, her friends or family, which was strange as the police report stated that she had been living there for about 18 months.

Terri headed out, tooting her horn to the security guard's wave as she passed through the gate. Well, it was time to really get this show on the road. First she would pay a visit to her contact at a major mobile phone company. She had tried calling all the numbers beside the strange names with the circle next to them. They were all no longer in service, except for one, which went straight to voicemail. Hopefully her contact would be able to tell her who the number belonged to.

⁂

Three hours after Meyers' kidnapping, the door to the room where he was being held opened slowly, and a tall, very dark man entered the room.

Jesus Christ! Meyers wondered if his swollen eyes were playing tricks on him. Upon entering the house, sandwiched between the two men, he had panicked and struggled with them. His futile struggle had lasted all of twenty five seconds. The result had been a battered face by fists that seemed to be made of granite.

He couldn't believe that the man standing in front of him was the person that had ordered his kidnapping.

He pulled up a chair in front of the one to which Meyers was tied, and sat his six foot four frame down with a grace unexpected from such a big man.

Meyers trembled, his eyes wide. What the fuck was really going on?

"I'm going to ask you a few questions," the man known as *Understanding* began conversationally. "And kindly confine your answers only to the questions asked." He paused and stared at Meyers intently.

"Why did Alexandra Fletcher come to see you?"

Meyers swallowed, his Adam's apple bobbing like it had a life of its own. Lord Jesus! What had he gotten himself into?

He told the man everything in a shaky voice.

The man nodded as he listened, a small smile tugging at the corners of his huge lips.

"What was in the package?" he asked, after Meyers had finished talking.

Meyers shook his head.

"I don't know. I never looked in it and as I said before, Superintendent Miller didn't open it in my presence," Meyers told him, maintaining eye contact in the hope that the man would see that he was telling the truth.

The man nodded again and stood up.

"I believe you," he said pleasantly, before turning and walking out the door, closing it behind him.

Meyers was so unnerved by the man that he was unable to control his bladder. The coffee and juice that he had consumed that morning darkened the front of his grey pants. An agonizingly long hour ticked by before he was untied and led back outside to the black SUV. None of the men commented on the obvious fact that he had peed himself. They left as they had arrived; Meyers sandwiched in the back between two men while another followed in Meyers' BMW sedan.

Meyers started to hope that they might release him. There was no one in Jamaica who would believe his story anyway. It was preposterous that *that* person would have kidnapped him so dramatically to question him about a dead prostitute's murder. It just didn't make any sense. But it had happened. He wasn't a particularly religious person but he prayed to God fervently that he would survive this weird and frightening ordeal.

CHAPTER 7

"Superintendent Miller!" Gilbert Chen gushed, when he saw the beautiful cop advancing towards his cubicle. "What a pleasant surprise."

Gilbert Chen was a diminutive twenty-four year old wonder geek. He was absolutely in love with Terri. Terri found him funny and adorable. He was also extremely helpful. She hoped that would be the case today.

She hugged him and sat down on the chair beside his desk. The office was abuzz with news of the popular cop's visit. Many of the employees, especially some of the guys, found all sorts of excuses to pass by Chen's cubicle. Terri was unperturbed by the attention. She was used to it.

"I need you to tell me who this number belongs to," Terri told him, handing him a post-it with the number on it.

"Sure," Chen said, typing in the number on his computer.

He frowned.

"Access is blocked," he said to Terri. "How important is this?"

"Very important," Terri said gravely, knowing he was about to hack into the account.

Chen nodded and worked his magic. Within five minutes he had hacked into the account.

"Gotcha!" he said triumphantly. "Someone went through a lot of trouble to restrict access to this account but they are no match for me."

Terri smiled gratefully.

"Ok, this number is registered to a Rebecca Smith," he told her.

Terri frowned. The name sounded oddly familiar.

"What's the address?" Terri asked.

"Jamaica Royal," Chen replied.

Terri was stunned.

Then she remembered. Rebecca Smith was the personal assistant of the Prime Minister.

What the hell was going on?

God was the Prime Minister?

CHAPTER 8

"Had a good trip?" Rebecca Smith asked her boss, the Prime Minister of Jamaica, as they relaxed in the backseat of the black Mercedes sedan. The sirens from the Prime Minister's police escort blared incessantly, though somewhat muted by the car's bullet proof windows.

"It was very fruitful," he responded, removing his spectacles and wiping his face with a white handkerchief. He had been away for four days on an official visit to the UK, meeting with the Jamaican Diaspora, doing radio and television interviews, and meeting with the British Prime Minister to discuss how both countries could help each other in these trying global times.

Interesting things had taken place in his absence. Alexandra Fletcher was dead. Without his sanctioning.

That was unacceptable. They were all influential and powerful men in their own right but he was the head honcho. He was *God*. The undisputed leader of The Circle. *Understanding*, who was in charge of security matters, had sent him an email advising him to terminate one of his mobile numbers. He had not done so. What for? There was no reason for that. Though he had three cell phones, he had begun using that number as his primary mobile number for about three months now. He wouldn't get rid of it without good reason.

The Circle would be meeting tonight at Jamaica Royal. These and other matters would be discussed.

❁❁❁❁❁❁❁❁❁

Understanding felt a lot better about the Terri Miller development. He still didn't know what was in the package that Alexandra Fletcher had left for her but when he got to that bridge, he would cross it. Everything else had been taken care of. He had possession of the dead woman's computer, all the phone numbers that the woman had used to contact The Circle were no longer in use, and the lawyer had been taken care of. There were no loopholes. Superintendent Miller's investigation would go nowhere. She would meet roadblocks at every juncture. She was the best but she was up against the kind of power that would crush her if she persisted. Dismissing her from his thoughts, he poured himself a shot of brandy and looked over the reports on his desk. He would be working late tonight. He wouldn't leave the office until it was time for the meeting at Jamaica Royal. He frowned at one of the reports.

That little prick.

⁕⁕⁕⁕⁕⁕

"Oh Lord Jesus Christ!" the nurse that was taking care of Meyers' mother whispered hoarsely as she looked at Meyers' body slumped over his steering wheel. He was obviously dead from a head wound. She had heard his car pull up in the driveway, but after ten minutes had passed without him coming inside to relieve her so that she could go home, she went outside to investigate. Crying, she staggered back inside to call the police.

⁕⁕⁕⁕⁕⁕

Detective Corporal Foster looked at the lawyer's dead body. He had been first on the scene along with two junior detectives. At first glance, it appeared to be a suicide. But something didn't make sense. The weapon, lying next to the dead man's feet, was a .38 revolver. It didn't have a silencer, yet no one in the quiet upscale complex had heard any shot being fired. He couldn't wait to get the ballistics report. He was willing to bet a month's pay that another weapon had been used and that this was no suicide. Plus the man, and his car, fitted the description of the gentleman who had been abducted from the parking lot of Police Headquarters. He watched as the new forensic specialist that the Jamaica Police Force had hired from Britain collect evidence from the undisturbed crime scene. He had already called Superintendent Miller and she was on her way. She was very interested in what he had told her.

✴✴✴✴✴✴✴✴

Terri arrived on the scene fifteen minutes after her conversation with Foster. She parked, waving to a well-dressed woman who had just arrived home from work and was staring curiously from across the street. The woman waved back with a tight smile. Terri went over to Foster, who was standing just inside the crime scene yellow tape talking on his phone. He wrapped up the conversation quickly.

"Superintendent Miller," he greeted warmly as he placed the phone inside his pocket.

"Hi," Terri replied, looking over grimly at the lawyer's dead body.

Foster brought her up to speed on everything as she listened attentively. Foster had learnt a lot from her over the years and owed his promotion to Detective Corporal to her. It was well-deserved. He was a very good cop. Had great cognitive skills, was highly intelligent and paid attention to detail.

Terri agreed that this was no suicide. His death had something to do with his visit to her and Alexandra Fletcher's death. She was sure of it. She implored the forensic specialist to hurry and get the ballistics test done on the gun. She wanted that report on her desk tonight. Terri then went inside the house to speak with the nurse and Meyers' sick mother.

The nurse, a sweet thirty-two year old mother of two, was understandably badly shaken but she managed to tell Terri all she knew. The mother, who suffered terribly from Alzheimer's, merely muttered 'Poor fellow' when she was advised of her son's death. She didn't know who they were talking about.

She issued some instructions to the constables on the scene and then left for Police Headquarters, telling Foster to meet her there.

She looked at the time as she headed down Constant Spring Road. It was now 5:30 p.m. She hadn't spoken to Marc-Anthony since dropping him off at school that morning. She sighed as she waited for Mavis, her longtime live-in helper, to answer the phone. The traffic was terrible. It would take her close to forty-five minutes to get to New Kingston.

"Hello," Mavis said on the fourth ring.

"Hi Mavis," Terri intoned. "Is everything ok at home?"

"Yes dear," she replied. "All is well. Your son is doing his homework."

"Let me speak to him."

Six seconds later, Marc-Anthony was on the line.

"Hi mom," he said brightly. "Coming home soon?"

Terri chuckled. She loved him so much. She didn't know what she would do if something ever happened to him.

"Hi baby. Not for another three hours. How was school today?"

"It was ok. I'm doing my homework."

Her son was no ordinary six year old. He was a brilliant child, advanced for his years.

"What is the assignment about?" Terri asked.

"I have to write an essay about what I want to be when I grow up and why."

"Ok I'll have a look at what you've done when I get home."

"Mom I'm waiting up for you tonight...no matter how late you get home," he said, adding cunningly, "I missed you very much today."

Terri laughed. Her son already had a way with the ladies.

"Until 10. If I don't get home by then you go to bed. Deal?"

"Yes, mom," he reluctantly agreed.

"I love you baby, bye."

Terri hung up and cursed under her breath at the slow moving traffic. She thought about *God's* shocking identity. The Prime Minister of Jamaica. She knew that Alexandra Fletcher's clientele was not comprised of ordinary men but that one had been a shocker. She would have to tread carefully and keep things close to the vest until she had found out exactly what was going on. But she was not afraid of investigating anyone, not even the Prime Minister, if they were guilty of wrongdoing.

She would be paying Jamaica Royal a visit sooner than later.

CHAPTER 9

Mrs. Roper was on her way home in her trusty station wagon when she heard the news on the radio. Her boss had been found dead in front of his home. The police had given a statement that for now it was being treated as a suicide. She hadn't been able to get him on his mobile since he left the office for his meeting with Superintendent Miller but this was the last thing she had expected to hear. Instinctively, she knew it wasn't a suicide. Martin Meyers would not have killed himself. She wouldn't believe that in a million years. She wondered, no *knew*, that it had something to do with those terrible people who had forced her to spy on him. Was she next? Her heart beat accelerated and her palms became sweaty. Oh God, no. What the hell had she done to deserve to be caught up in this sordid mess? She drove home in a daze.

Gilbert Chen left the office at 6 p.m. that evening. He bobbed his head as he listened to the sounds of rock band Blink 182 on his iPod. He got to his car and was about to open the door when he was grabbed from behind. He screamed into a man's huge hand as he struggled mightily, before his attacker, seemingly tired of struggling with the surprisingly strong pint-sized Chinese geek, slashed his throat and threw him down onto the ground. The man quickly removed Chen's iPod and wallet, which he emptied of the few dollars he found, and threw the wallet on the ground next to Chen's twitching body. He then removed the car radio and DVD player, took Chen's laptop and cell phone, and satisfied that it looked like a robbery, hopped into a waiting SUV and exited the parking lot.

Seven minutes later, three of Chen's co-workers came around the corner and were about to pile into the Toyota Camry owned by one of them, when the chubby technician who worked a few cubicles down from Chen, saw the gruesome scene. He vomited his late lunch of home cooked rice and peas and roast beef while another ran back inside the office to call the police.

※※※※※※※※

"Wow, the Prime Minister?" Foster echoed, as he slouched on a chair in Terri's office. Terri had told him about the dead prostitute and Martin Meyers' connection to her, as well as everything that she had found out thus far.

"Yep," Terri said, taking a sip of her bottled water. "I can't wait to find out what his moniker means in relation to the other nine strange names with the circles beside them. I'm positive it's important and has serious bearing on whatever is going on."

Foster looked at the list of names thoughtfully.

"Yeah, you're probably right...as usual." He smiled at Terri. He was still, after all these years, very much taken by her but still could not work up the nerve to say something about the way that he felt. Most of the time he was glad he hadn't, as it would have probably made things a bit awkward between them – at least on his part – but other times he wished that he could just get it off his chest. "So what's our next move?"

Terri was about to answer him when her mobile rang.

Her face went ashen.

She terminated the call and rose, grabbing her pocket book.

"Gilbert Chen, the computer geek who found out the Prime Minister's identity was murdered," she told Foster as she went through the door quickly with Foster on her heels.

Terri sighed as they hurriedly made their way to the parking lot.

The bodies were piling up at an alarming rate.

There was no way she was going to make it home before Marc-Anthony's bedtime.

CHAPTER 10

"Why wasn't I informed that there was still one of the numbers in operation?" *Understanding* demanded. He was at his office, his shiny boots ensconced on his large desk, as he bellowed into the phone. He had given his contact at the mobile phone company strict instructions to delete all information concerning the ten numbers that belonged to the members of The Circle, and he had done that, except for one. And now Terri Miller, because of that shit-head geek, knew the identity of *God*. It wasn't a major problem that couldn't be dealt with but it should not have happened. It placed the Prime Minister in an embarrassing light and compromised the highest office of the land, but that would be the extent of the damage. Terri Miller would find out nothing more. Absolutely *nothing*.

"Bu-bu-t..." the man sputtered, cursing himself for not doing as he was told. *Understanding* was not someone to be played with. But it was just that the number belonged to the *Prime Minister*. He didn't want to delete it until he had gotten a confirmation from Rebecca Smith, the Prime Minister's beautiful dragon of an assistant. She was a balls-breaking bitch and the last thing he needed was her embarrassing him or worse, getting him fired. He had thought that he would have gotten the confirmation in due course, delete the number and all its corresponding information, and all would be well. But all wasn't well. When he had contacted her, Rebecca had told him to leave the fucking number alone because the Prime Minister was going to keep it and now he was in big trouble.

"Just shut your mouth! You stammering idiot!" *Understanding* thundered. "I'll deal with you some other time."

He slammed the phone down and drained his brandy, his third shot of the evening. He just *hated* when people couldn't follow simple instructions. Asshole. He needed to blow off some steam. He picked up the phone and buzzed his personal assistant.

She entered the room and looked at him questioningly.

"Strip!" he ordered.

She quickly did as she was told, her heart filled with fear and hatred, and bent over his desk, just the way he liked it.

Keeping his clothes on, he unzipped his pants and pulled out his hard dick through his fly and rolled on a condom. He then positioned himself behind her and entered her dryness with a brutal thrust.

Tears streamed down her eyes as she grunted with each thrust. She couldn't deal with this anymore.

Today was the last time.

Even if she had to take her own life.

❈❈❈❈❈❈❈

Terri felt really bad about Gilbert Chen's murder. She felt personally responsible. Her eyes brimmed with tears as she looked at the grotesque scene. If he hadn't helped her, he would still be alive. She was positive that robbery was not the motive for his murder, it was simply a distraction. They must have found out that he had hacked into the account and killed him. These people were not playing around. And neither was she. She was sure that by now the Prime Minister had been alerted that his identity had been compromised. Did he give the order for Chen's execution? This was heavy stuff and getting heavier by the minute. And she had yet to brief her mentor and boss, Police Commissioner Erwin Baxter. She would have to meet with him no later than tomorrow. The ramifications of the Prime Minister being the subject of a murder investigation ran far and deep. He was one of the most the respected Caribbean leaders on the world stage. If he was indeed eventually arrested and charged, the fallout would be almost catastrophic. Already deemed one of the most corrupt nations in the world, the country's reputation would endure a significant battering.

It was a very complex situation but people were being murdered.

Justice had to be served.

CHAPTER 11

Terri finally got home at 11:30 p.m. It had been a brutal day. She was tired but she couldn't stop thinking about the case. She had gotten back the ballistics report from the gun used in the Meyers shooting and it was as she had surmised. The gun found in his hand was not the gun used to kill him. She deduced that he was shot by someone in the passenger seat of his car, with a nine millimeter pistol equipped with a silencer. Meyers was right-handed yet the bullet had entered from the left side of his head.

Terri switched off the living room light which Mavis had left on for her, and went into the kitchen where she had some of the beef soup that Mavis had cooked for dinner. She then went to Marc-Anthony's room. She sat on his bed and looked at his sleeping form in the semi-darkness. She was about to kiss him when he jumped up and growled, startling her.

"You little devil!" Terri shrieked in laughter. "You scared me."

Marc-Anthony laughed and hugged her.

"Why aren't you sleeping young man...instead of being up trying to give your poor mother a heart attack," Terri said as she lovingly stroked his curly hair.

"I just woke up mom," he protested, his unusual grey eyes twinkling mischievously in the low light.

"Liar!" Terri growled as she tickled him mercilessly. She didn't stop until he apologized for scaring her. She kissed him.

"Did you finish your assignment?"

"Yeah, Mom. How was work?"

"Hectic. Mommy is so tired."

He hugged her tightly.

"Ok then go get some rest."

Terri chuckled. Her little man. God she loved him. Though she had discovered that he had a half brother close to three years ago, she had yet to tell him. She still had not come to terms with the fact that Anthony had fathered another child with someone else, round about the *same* time that he had gotten her pregnant. That showed her that she still wasn't completely over him but she was getting there. At least the nightmares had stopped. She hadn't had one in almost two years. She suspected that being with Nico also helped in that regard.

"Good night baby."

"Good night Mom."

She left the room and softly closed the door behind her.

⁕⁕⁕⁕⁕⁕⁕⁕⁕

Forty-five minutes later, after a bubble bath, pistachio ice cream and soothing classical music, Terri was in bed wearing one of Nico's T-shirts. She had taken three of them from his home in Queens precisely for moments like these, when she missed him more than usual. She picked up the cordless phone and dialed his mobile.

"Hi baby," he cooed, answering on the third ring. "I was just thinking about you."

"Is that right," Terri drawled, already feeling horny at the mere sound of his voice. "What are you up to?"

"I just took a shower. I got in a few minutes ago... attended an album release party," he replied, sitting on the bed with a plush black towel wrapped around his waist.

Terri groaned audibly at the thought of his chiseled, still slightly wet frame just getting out of the shower. It had been over two months since they last saw each other. He was supposed to be coming to Jamaica in three weeks but with the way this new case was going, it was possible that she might have to wait until it was over to see him.

"What's wrong baby?" Nico asked, hearing her torturous groan.

"I want you," she whispered hoarsely, "so bad..."

Nico could feel an erection on the way. He was positive that he was going to marry Terri one day. There wasn't another woman alive that could make him feel the way she did.

"Oh baby...I want you too...I'm getting hard right now...are you wet? Touch my pussy and tell me if it's wet..."

"Jesus Christ...Nico...don't do this to me..." she pleaded as she moved her free hand down to her vagina. She was extremely wet.

"It's soaked baby...crying for you..." she told him as she rubbed her clitoris, which had begun to throb unbearably.

"Play with my pussy baby...tell her how much I miss her...slip a finger inside and stroke her for me..." he instructed.

"Ohhhh...Nico...mmmm..." Terri moaned as she did as she was told, her finger moving in and out with wild abandon.

"Stroke it for me boo...now put your finger in your mouth."

Terri removed her index finger, now slick with her juices, and placed it inside her mouth, sucking it hungrily.

"Now play with your clit baby...picture me inside you...fucking you deep from behind...making you climax over and over again...calling out my name until you're hoarse..."

Terri grunted as he whispered sweet, nasty nothings into the phone, her hand moving rapidly against her turgid clit as she sought release, his voice and words urging her on to ecstasy.

"I'm coming baby...I'm coming...it's right there... Nico! Nico! Nico!" Terri breathed through clenched teeth, trying to keep her voice down as her orgasm gripped her body and shook it like a rag doll.

"Thank you baby...I needed that," she said breathlessly. "It has been a long eventful day...now I can sleep like a baby."

Nico chuckled.

"Lucky you...now I've got a big problem to tackle," he quipped.

"Hush baby...at least you've got the video," she replied. It had taken him some doing to convince her to allow him to record one of their lovemaking sessions. But the video was so hot. It was exciting watching herself in action to say the least.

"That I do," he agreed. "I'll pop it in and take care of this as soon as I finish talking to you."

"So what's happening with work?" Nico asked.

"Well I've got this new case working on," she replied through a yawn, feeling very comfortable and sleepy now. Nothing like some TLC from the one you love to seep away the day's stress, even if it was over the phone. "It's shaping up to be a nasty one."

"Ok, well be careful baby," he said. "I know you can take care of yourself but you've got two men who need you."

Terri smiled. Yes she did. She hoped that Marc-Anthony would like Nico. After all, she was thinking that he was the one. He would be around for a very long time, God willing.

"I will baby," she assured him.

"So whose album release party did you go to? One of your artistes?" she asked.

"Underground rapper named Knowledge Supreme. He's really good...hard hitting conscious rhymes. He's not my artiste but I dig his music and a good friend of mine is his manager."

"Knowledge Supreme...unusual name," Terri commented.

"Yeah...he's a member of the Five Percent Nation, a quasi-religious group," Nico explained. "They study Mathematics. Numbers have meanings in their teachings. For example, one means knowledge, two means understanding and three means equality."

Terri sat up in bed with a jolt.

"What does four and five mean?" Her brain was swirling.

"Ummm...I don't recall the meaning of four but five means power," Nico told her.

She got out of bed and booted up her computer.

"Ok, baby, sounds cool," she said. "Have a good night and I'll talk to you tomorrow."

"Ok boo, I love you. Sleep tight."

"Love you too baby."

Terri terminated the call and quickly googled the Five Percent Nation.

She scrolled through the information and sure enough, the names on the list that was in Alexandra Fletcher's little black book corresponded with the meanings of the numbers in the Five Percent Nation doctrine.

Why would they name themselves after a street-oriented quasi religious cult? Well at least now she knew where they got the names from and based on the meanings of the names, she had a nagging suspicion that the person named *Born*, which corresponded with the number nine, was a woman.

She bookmarked the web page, turned off the computer and went back to bed. She thought about the case until her brain finally shut down and she fell asleep.

CHAPTER 12

Understanding was in a foul mood as he headed home from the meeting at Jamaica Royal, sitting in the back of a black Range Rover, his personal vehicle. His driver, sensing his mood, refrained from making small talk. The Prime Minister had pissed him off, making a big deal about the murder of the prostitute and everything that had happened since. He had snapped at him, letting him know that there was nothing to worry about as he had it all under control, while the other members of the circle had looked on stoically, used to the power struggle between the two of them.

The Circle was *Understanding's* brainchild. He had conceptualized the creation of a secret body, comprised of powerful people from different sectors of the Jamaican society, who collectively would amass even greater wealth and power, and shape the way the country was run. He had carefully identified nine others and approached them individually, convincing them of the viability of his plan. They had all been interested and on a rainy Saturday night, at a villa in Ocho Rios owned by *Understanding*, The Circle was born.

In four short years they had accomplished a lot by pooling their resources. They had played a great role in getting the current Prime Minister elected in the last general election and figuratively, he was considered the head of The Circle but everyone knew that *Understanding* and not *God*, was the real leader, when it came down to it. And it wasn't all business. Any sexual vice, however vile or illegal, was provided to any member who required it. They lived above the law, and in some instances, *were* the law. They were untouchable. Terri Miller would soon realize that. She was in way over her head. She just didn't know it yet.

He glanced at his Rolex watch. It was 2 a.m. He removed a small vial of cocaine from his inner jacket pocket. He took two sniffs and within seconds, felt rejuvenated. There were two women at his home, waiting for him. High class hookers who would per-form whatever act he required. He thought of Alexandra Fletcher as the vehicle turned on to Hill Run road. He was almost home. He missed her. He had never met anyone like her. Too bad things had ended the way they did. She had been very good at her job. The best. His mood improved considerably by the time he entered the house and went upstairs where the two negligee clad women were relaxing in the bedroom he used to conduct sessions like this. The room was filled with sex furniture such as Zeppelin and Liberator Esse pieces, toys of all shapes and sizes, and had mirrored walls and ceiling.

He looked at the women critically as he undressed. His assistant charged with the duty of procuring women to satisfy his vast lust had chosen well. They looked like beautiful models. One very dark, the other extremely light skinned. He liked the contrast.

He had taken his Viagra two and a half hours ago.

He was rearing to go.

It was going to be a long and painful night.

He hoped they were up for it.

CHAPTER 13

Terri got in at 9:15 a.m. after dropping off Marc-Anthony at school. She always tried to take him to school whenever possible as she hardly ever got the opportunity to pick him up in the evenings. A very understanding and sage child, he knew that his mom had an important and demanding job so he never fussed when he was taken home by the armed driver that Terri had hired to transport him. Today was Thursday, that meant he had karate lessons after school. Terri greeted Mrs. Green and went inside her office. She closed the door behind her and sorted out some paperwork until her 9:45 meeting with Detective Corporal Foster. He was very excited about something that he wanted to show her.

Mrs. Roper finished cleaning out her desk and looked around the office where she had worked for the past six years one last time. Her boss was dead and she was suddenly out of a job. Being unemployed in a recession was not going to be easy. Thankfully her husband's job was relatively secure and Janice, her daughter, was in her final year at university. She locked the door and handed over the key to the caretaker. She then made her way to her car, looking around nervously. The horrible men that had forced her to spy on her boss had not contacted her since his death but that had done nothing to help her paranoia. She still wondered if they would harm her. It was stressful not knowing their intentions.

She decided to go and see Raymond, the twenty-three year old college student that she had been having an affair with for the past nine months. He had only one class today and wouldn't be leaving home until 3:30 p.m. That gave her loads of time to get some loving – two rounds would be good – before going home to cook dinner. She had given the helper time off indefinitely to cut costs seeing as she would be home now and could assume the household responsibilities. She headed out of the RDC parking lot for what she was sure would be the last time, and turned onto Holborn Road. It had been a subconscious decision as she hadn't planned on going to see Raymond, but she was happy that she selected her red g-string this morning.

Red was his favourite colour.

Terri looked at the sketch for several prolonged seconds. Foster was right. The drawing, done from Foster's notes containing the eyewitness' description of one of the men that had kidnapped Martin Meyers in the parking lot of Police Headquarters, resembled Detective Corporal Sheldon Jackson, a senior detective attached to ECU, the Elite Crimes Unit, which was under the direct supervision of the Police Commissioner himself. Terri frowned. Ever since its inception three years ago, the ECU had been mired in controversy after controversy. One reporter had likened them to the KGB, the former Soviet Union's secret police. Though their methods were questionable – they rarely ever brought in anyone they accosted alive – and they operated under a cloak of secrecy and seemingly without impunity, they got results, and as the Police Commissioner loved to point out to the Unit's detractors, numbers never lie.

"It's him," Foster reiterated with conviction. "The nose alone would give him away. It's the biggest nose in the Police Force."

Terri chuckled wryly.

"This case stinks," Terri commented, her eyes now serious. "I have a meeting with the Commissioner this afternoon. I'm going to discuss everything with him before I take any action. Don't approach Jackson. I will deal with him."

Foster nodded. He wouldn't have gotten anywhere anyway. Jackson was backed by the Police Commissioner himself. He would have most likely told Foster to go fuck himself. Superintendent Miller would have to be the one. She commanded almost as much respect as the Police Commissioner. Jackson would *have* to talk to her.

Terri leaned back in her chair and glanced at the photo of her parents on her desk as Foster exited her office. Her relationship with her parents, which had become very strained due to their reaction when she had gotten pregnant out of wedlock and would not divulge the identity of the father, had pretty much gotten back to normal when she was in Miami recuperating after her near death experience with the *Wolf Man* three years ago. That was when she had forgiven them, beginning with her mom who had stayed in Miami with her the entire time, and then her father, when she retuned to Jamaica.

Though they were close again, she still hadn't told them about Nico yet, but she planned on Nico meeting them when he got to Jamaica in three weeks. She couldn't wait to see him. Her intercom beeped, breaking her out of her reverie. She answered it. Mrs. Green told her that there was a call for her on the line but the person, other than saying that it was extremely urgent, wouldn't identify himself.

Mildly curious, Terri took the call.

"Forget about the case. It's no use to pursue it. You will get nowhere. Back off bitch. Consider this your first and only warning," a slightly muffled voice said before hanging up.

Terri was bemused as she slowly hung up the phone.

You don't say. We'll see about that Mister.

CHAPTER 14

"**R**aymond! Raymond!" Mrs. Roper called out irritably, standing on the verandah of the house where Raymond resided in Mona Commons with his mother and younger sister. She knew he was home as she had heard low music and voices when she arrived. The voices had stopped after she started calling out his name when he wouldn't answer his phone. The music was still playing though.

She banged on the door.

"Raymond! I know you're in there! Open the door!" she demanded, growing increasingly angry by the second.

A woman, a domestic worker for the couple who lived next door, was hanging out clothes on the line. She watched interestedly as the drama unfolded, happy that the monotony of her day was broken. Mrs. Roper saw her but simply treated her to a dirty look and kept on banging on the door.

"Just a minute," she heard Raymond call out from inside.

She continued to bang anyway until he opened the door.

He came out onto the verandah and closed the door behind him. He was clad in a pair of shorts and his body was shiny with perspiration.

He rubbed his eyes and yawned, as though just awakening.

"Why yuh out here making up so much noise Karen?" he asked irritably. "I was in my deep sleep and next thing this loud noise just wake me up."

Mrs. Roper looked at the young man that was twenty years her junior with an angry, suspicious glare.

"Why are you so sweaty?" she asked loudly, her hands on her hips. "And why aren't you inviting me in? I didn't come here to stand up on your verandah and chit chat."

"Yuh nuh see how the time hot?" Raymond exclaimed. "I fell asleep without turning on the fan. No yuh can't come in right now Karen. If you had called and let me know that you were planning on coming by I would have told you no because my mom didn't go to work today. She went to the doctor and she'll soon be home."

This *boy* thought that she was stupid.

She pushed him aside and entered the house before he could stop her.

Raymond could hear the nosy helper next door erupting in laughter as he ran inside after Mrs. Roper.

⚜⚜⚜⚜⚜⚜

"How are you Terri?" Erwin Baxter, the Police Commissioner asked, treating her to a paternal gaze as they sat inside his office.

"I'm fine," she replied with a smile. Baxter was her mentor, and had played a great role in getting her promoted through the ranks fairly, based on her skill and performance on the job, as opposed to the usual old boys club mentality which plagued most male-dominated professions. She hadn't gotten any thing that she didn't deserve or worked hard for, but she appreciated everything that he had done for her.

"And the little one?" he asked, reaching for the remote control and turning down the air conditioner. He liked the room to feel ice cold but he knew that most people would feel uncomfortable. Terri was grateful for the respite. Her nipples had begun to harden.

"He's great," she told him. She had never discussed her son with the Police Commissioner, or anyone other than her family and close friends for that matter, but he always asked about him.

"So...what is this important matter that you wish to discuss?" he asked, ready to begin. He arrived at the office at midday and his secretary had handed him Terri's urgent request for a meeting. He had dealt with a few matters and an hour later, sent for her.

"Yes," Terri began, opening a thin file as she handed him an identical one. "It's about Alexandra Fletcher, the prostitute that was found dead the other day."

He nodded, prompting her to go on.

She did, beginning with Martin Meyers' visit to her and ending with the warning she had received to drop the case.

"My God," Baxter said when she had finished. "This is heavy Terri. Very heavy."

He got up and went over to the window behind his desk and looked down on the scores of corporate employees scurrying up and down Knutsford Boulevard as they made their way to and from lunch.

"We have to tread very carefully," he advised gravely, turning around to face her. "I'll call the Prime Minister myself and set up the meeting. It would be best if I contact him personally."

He perched on the edge of his desk.

"This stays at the highest level Terri. I'm the only person that you're to discuss this case with and I want updates as soon as they become available. As for

Detective Corporal Jackson, the witness was mistaken. He was in my office at the time of the kidnapping."

Terri mulled over that unexpected bit of information. The woman had gotten a good view of the man she had described. She had seen four men but had only gotten a good enough look at one of them, the one that had approached Meyers with the taser. The one that looked exactly like Jackson, down to the large, snout-like nose that Jackson possessed. It was a big blow as she had been looking forward to interrogate Jackson. But if the Commissioner himself was Jackson's alibi, what could she say?

"Ok sir, thanks much and I'll keep you updated." She took up her file and rose, feeling disappointed. "Enjoy the rest of the day and we'll talk soon."

"Ok Terri, and don't worry about the threat...I doubt anyone would be stupid enough to try and harm you but you never know...so be careful until we get to the bottom of this thing, ok?"

She nodded and turned to leave.

"By the way," he said, stopping her in mid-stride. "Was Fletcher's computer ever found?"

"No sir," Terri replied, her heart pounding loudly.

He waved bye and she smiled weakly and exited his office, closing the door softly behind her.

The Police Commissioner's personal assistant, a pretty, shapely young lady with sad eyes, looked up at Terri as she walked by. For a moment it appeared as though she was about to say something but changed her mind and averted her eyes, looking intently at her computer screen.

Terri walked down the corridor to her office – it was on the same floor as that of the Commissioner and the Deputy Commissioner – and went inside, immediately buzzing Mrs. Green and advising her that she was not to be disturbed.

She got a bottle of water from the small refrigerator and sat down heavily.

She had not mentioned anything about Alexandra Fletcher's missing computer in her report to the Commissioner and as far she knew, this was the first time he was hearing the details about the case.

Yet he had mentioned it.

How did he know that the computer was missing?

Terri dreaded the answer.

❈❈❈❈❈❈❈❈

Mrs. Roper charged through the living room and made her way down the passage to Raymond's bedroom.

"Karen! Karen!" Raymond called out as he caught up with her and held on to her hand.

She shrugged him off and opened his bedroom door.

A young woman was in the process of pulling on a pair of very tight jeans. She froze and looked up, her large firm breasts jutting provocatively, the nipples rock hard, still in a state of arousal.

She stared at the young woman angrily.

The girl, who knew about Raymond's relationship with the older *married* woman, stared back defiantly as she resumed pulling up her jeans.

"What the fuck are you looking at?" she challenged, looking at Mrs. Roper up and down with a scornful look on her face as if to say how Raymond could even stomach to touch that.

Mrs. Roper did not accept the challenge. It would not be her finest moment getting into a fight with a girl younger than her own daughter, and over a man no less. The situation was bad enough.

"So this is how you treat me after all that I've done for you?" she demanded, shaking her head tearfully and walking out of the room.

Raymond gestured to the girl to stay put inside the room and went out behind Mrs. Roper.

"Karen...it's not like that...but you just pop up on me...I have a life too yuh know," he said in a conciliatory tone. "Yuh have your husband...I couldn't just show up at *your* house like this....so why I can't get the same respect?"

"You ungrateful fucker," Mrs. Roper spat. "Look how much I've spent on you. Eh? Paid your school fee for this semester, bought you clothes...and this is the thanks I get? Fuck you Raymond!"

She pushed past him and stumbled out into the bright sunlight, making her way tearfully to her car.

Laughter rang in her ears as the woman next door cackled loudly.

She had never been so embarrassed in her life.

CHAPTER 15

Terri left work earlier than usual that evening. She was very unsettled. She kept telling herself that there must be a reasonable explanation as to how the Police Commissioner knew about Alexandra Fletcher's missing computer. There *must* be. The alternative was unthinkable. There was also the matter of Jackson being in the Commissioner's office at the time of the kidnapping. Terri had a gut feeling that the Commissioner was lying. And her instincts were *never* wrong. It was a lot to wrap her head around but she needed to get a handle on things and decide how to proceed from here on out. She felt a presence as she approached her vehicle and turned around, her free hand inching close to the holstered firearm underneath her jacket. She was in a state of heightened paranoia. Nothing was as it seemed and she had to expect the unexpected. Cliché but so true.

It was the Police Commissioner's personal assistant. She was new. Had only been on the job for about three weeks. He changed them often. The one prior to her had lasted only a month.

Terri looked at her questioningly. She was about to open her mouth to speak when her mobile rang. She looked at the caller ID and visibly trembled.

"Hello," she said, her small voice coated with despair and fear.

Terri watched her closely, very concerned and curious as to what was going on with the young lady.

"Yes," she said resignedly, after listening for several seconds.

She looked mournfully at Terri and for the second time that day, whatever she wanted to say died in her throat. She turned abruptly and swiftly made her way back inside the building.

Terri watched her retreating back, unsure if she should go after her and demand her to tell her what was happening. The poor girl was deathly afraid of something or somebody, and if she was in trouble, it was Terri's job to assist. She felt eyes on her and looked up. Someone was looking at her from the narrow but long window at the end of the passage on the eleventh floor. She couldn't see the person's face but she could tell that it was a man, dressed in full black.

The person made a threatening gesture, moving a solitary finger across his neck, mimicking a throat being slashed before moving away.

Terri's eyes narrowed. The person was making a clear reference to her near death experience five years ago when her throat was slashed by a dangerous psychopath.

If the Wolf Man couldn't do it you damn sure can't, Terri mused as she went inside her vehicle.

Battle lines were drawn.

She had enemies inside the Police Force.

That they could be operating under the instructions of the man that she most respected and admired in the world other than her father, and more recently Barack Obama, was unnerving to say the least.

Given his position, it was downright frightening and demoralizing.

She gunned the engine and headed out of the parking lot.

She couldn't wait to get home, hang out with Marc-Anthony for a bit, then retire to the privacy of her room with that treasured unopened bottle of Remy Martin Louis XIII.

Lord knows she needed a drink.

"Hi Mom!" Marc-Anthony greeted enthusiastically when Terri got home. He was in the living room, sitting on the plush carpet in front of the seventy-two inch plasma T.V. playing Ghostbusters on his Xbox 360. He paused the game and hopped up to hug his mother. "You're home early."

Terri kissed him.

"Yes I am, how's my baby?"

"I'm ok." Then his twinkling unusual eyes got serious. "I have something to tell you."

Terri looked at him, suddenly worried.

"What is it baby?" she asked.

"I met someone today," he replied, his voice now several octaves lower.

"Who?"

Marc-Anthony looked at her for a moment before responding. His grey eyes were faintly accusing.

"My brother," he replied softly.

His mother's eyes bulged in shock.

Terri took a deep breath. How the hell did this happen? She had wanted to speak to Marc-Anthony about it when she was ready. After she had sorted it all out in her head. And after four years, she still hadn't. But no such luck. Somehow, fate had intervened and now she had some damage control to do. She led him by hand to his room and closed the door.

"Tell me what happened," she said softly, sitting beside him on the bed.

"There's a new student in my karate class...he looks just like me. Exactly like me mom," he emphasized, sounding excited and confused. "Everybody kept asking us if we were brothers but he didn't say anything and neither did I."

Terri squeezed his hand reassuringly and he continued.

When he was through, Terri looked at the card that the woman, the other child's mother, had given Marc-Anthony to give to her. It was her husband's business card and had her mobile number written on the back. Terri had met the good doctor a few years ago when she was working on the *Wolf Man* case. She never forgot how she had felt when she saw the family picture of the doctor, his wife and their son, and realized that it was true that Anthony had fathered a child with another woman. She still hadn't gotten over it and as such, had yet to discuss it with Marc-Anthony. Now her hand was forced. Perhaps it was God's way of letting her know that she was wrong to keep the brothers apart.

She looked at Marc-Anthony. He was watching her, his beautiful grey eyes asking a million questions.

Choosing her words carefully, she answered them as best she could.

CHAPTER 16

Maria was applying the finishing touches to dinner when her mobile vibrated loudly on the kitchen counter. Today they were having lamb, fried potatoes and *arroz cubano* – a mound of white rice topped with tomato sauce and a fried egg. Though she had been living in Jamaica for almost seven years now, she still liked to cook her Spanish dishes along with the traditional Jamaican food that her husband loved so much. It was important to her that Diego, her son, learn about that side of his heritage. He spoke Spanish as fluently as he did English, as she had ensured that he was taught both. From his perch on a stool, he watched as his mother wiped her hands on her apron and answered the phone.

"Hello," she said in accented English.

"Hi, Maria?"

"Yes, this is she," Maria replied, looking at Diego. He had been moody ever since he discovered that he had a brother. She had a long talk with him when they got home but he had been very quiet. She had no idea what was going on in his head. He was so much like his father. He could be very moody and cold at times.

"This is Terri. You met my son today."

Maria sighed with relief. She was hoping that the woman would have accepted her gesture and called. It wasn't fair for the brothers to be kept apart. It had been an emotional scene at the karate class today. When she arrived and took Diego over to the instructor, he had looked at the gathering of twenty young boys and ten girls intently. Maria had followed his gaze and almost fainted when she saw who he was gazing at. His brother. Unexpectedly seeing Anthony's other child had threatened to overwhelm her as the discovery of him six years ago had done when he was just a baby. Now he was the same age as Diego and they were practically identical. He stared back at Diego too, his eyes blazing in shock and confusion.

"I didn't know that Marc-Anthony had a brother," the instructor had commented, his high pitch voice sounding even higher in his surprise. Marc-Anthony Miller had been taking karate lessons for three months now and sometimes, though rarely, his mother, the celebrity cop, would pick him up. But this child had a different mother so they obviously shared the same dad and they were the same age. *What a prekeh!* The man mused inwardly, looking forward to going home to gossip with his live in lover.

Maria had ignored him and sat down in a daze with the other parents who had stayed to watch their kids. When the session ended, Maria asked permission from the stony-faced, well dressed man who was taking Marc-Anthony out to the parking lot if she could speak with him for a second.

She had quickly scribbled her number on the card and asked him to give it to the child's mother. Expressionless, he had agreed and without a word, had placed Marc-Anthony inside the back of an SUV and taken him home.

Diego had listened intently to everything that she told him but did not comment afterwards. Three and a half hours later, he still hadn't. He was not the kind of child that she could badger to talk when he didn't want to, she had to wait until he was ready. Her husband had tried on several occasions in the past to use force and punishment in getting him to speak up when something was bothering him but that had failed miserably. Only his mother could deal with him when he was like this.

"Thank you so much for calling," Maria said. "We really need to talk."

Terri took a deep breath and exhaled. *This was the other woman.* The woman that the love of her life had been with simultaneously. The woman in which the love of her life had deposited his seed, leaving her with the same precious gift that he had left with Terri, that of a child.

The pain had not gone away. It had only remained dormant, biding its time underneath the surface. And now, it had erupted, bringing with it vivid bitter sweet memories of her brief but dramatic relationship with Anthony, the man she had loved but had had to kill.

"Yes, we do. How about tonight?" Terri suggested. Now was as good a time as any. It had been a very emotional day in many ways. Might as well do this while she was already in emotional turmoil.

"Sure," Maria agreed readily. "Any time after 7 p.m. Where would you like to meet?"

By then her husband, who had quit the hospital and had a private practice for the last two years, would be home and she could give him his dinner before leaving.

Terri thought for a moment. Had to be somewhere where they could talk without being overheard.

"Ok, meet me at Devon House at 7:45. Take my mobile number and call me when you get there."

Maria scribbled Terri's mobile number on the pst-it on the kitchen counter and hung up after thanking her again for calling. She ran a hand through Diego's curly mane and gave him a kiss. She then shared his dinner.

Soon he would be hurt and confused no more. He would have his brother in his life.

Just the way it should be.

CHAPTER 17

Detective Corporal Jackson drained the last of his scotch, smacked his lips appreciatively and placed the glass on the small trolley beside his boss' desk.

"You think she'll really back off?" he queried skeptically as he glanced at his watch. It was 7 p.m. He was getting hungry. He wondered what his wife had cooked for dinner. That was the main reason he had married her. Her culinary skills were second to none. After the first meal she had cooked for him two years ago, he knew that he would never let her go.

"She'll have no choice," *Understanding* replied confidently, as he poured himself another shot of brandy. "When you meet up in a brick wall that you can't go through or go over, you have only two choices. Either you turn back or you just stop. Either way, you cannot proceed."

They were in his office at Police Headquarters, having a late evening drink while they discussed the Terri Miller situation. She was like a daughter to him. The best cop he had ever seen. But he wouldn't hesitate to kill her if it came down to it. If things were allowed to get out of hand the result would be catastrophic. This was bigger than Terri Miller. Bigger than a dead whore. The Circle had to go on about its business unimpeded. Too much was at stake.

"Ok boss," Jackson said agreeably. Terri Miller was a formidable foe but she could be handled. He didn't like her. Despised her in fact. She was always showing up everybody else in the force, acting like she was the only one blessed with intelligence, always hogging the spotlight and the glory. She was a fucking hypocrite. Always acting like she cared so much about her country and the people when she was nothing but a rich, narcissistic cunt who loved being in the limelight. Everyone knew that she had her eye on the Police Commissioner's job. Imagine that. The day that cunt became Police Commissioner would be his last day as a cop.

There was nothing more he would love than for the boss to give the go ahead to terminate her. He would do it in fine style. Have his way with her before sending her screaming into eternity. He hoped that she would continue to make trouble. Then she would get exactly what's coming to her. He knew she was close to the Commissioner but he had been working directly for him long enough to know that he would get rid of her if she pushed hard enough. Nothing or no one got in the way of The Circle.

He remembered the first time the Commissioner had taken him in his confidence and told him about The Circle. It had blown his mind. He had thought that things like that only existed in the movies and in novels. But it was happening. Right here in Jamaica. They were the ones who really ran the country. It was the day that he knew that he had proven himself and was now an integral part of the Commissioner's team. Who knows, maybe one day he would be a member of The Circle himself.

✦✦✦✦✦✦✦✦

"Hello," Terri said, answering on the second ring. She was sitting in her SUV in the parking lot of Devon House, a popular hang out spot for ice cream and a Kingston landmark. People were always there, but Terri chose it because it was a vast property, and they could easily find a private spot to talk. She had just seen a black Toyota Prado pull up in a parking spot a few meters away. It wasn't tinted and she could see the driver. A pretty Hispanic woman. Instinctively, she knew that it was Maria. She was right.

"Hi Terri, it's Maria," Maria said. "I just arrived."

"I see you," Terri said. "I'll come over."

Terri hung up and taking a deep breath, grabbed her tote bag and exited the vehicle. She was casually dressed in jeans, loafers and a form fitting sweater. She walked over to Maria who was now anxiously standing beside her vehicle.

"Hi," Terri said simply, extending her hand.

Maria shook it.

"Hi," she replied, surprised etched on her pretty features. "It's you...oh my God."

She had seen Terri on numerous occasions on T.V. and in the newspapers. She was the cop that had killed Anthony. Maria felt faint.

Terri looked around. Too many people were milling about.

"Follow me," she instructed and walked off, expecting Maria to follow. She did, on legs that suddenly felt inadequate to carry her modest weight.

Terri led her over to the far end of the lawn away from everyone. The closest person to them, a teenage couple who were sharing an ice cream cone, was over 200 meters away. They sat on the grass facing each other.

"You killed him," Maria whispered hoarsely, her voice filled with so much pain that it was as if Anthony had just died.

Terri looked at her coldly.

"If you are in so much pain then imagine what I went through...and is still going through," Terri told her in a steely tone. "Discovering that the man I loved is a criminal and being forced to kill him. You think that shit was a walk in the park?"

Terri blinked back tears as she spoke, trying not to break down in front of this woman, who was already crying.

"Then to top it off I discover by chance, in the middle of a most difficult and emotional investigation, that he had fathered another child with someone else. The entire experience gave me nightmares for several years."

Her Blackberry Bold vibrated. She looked at it. It was an email from Anna. Terri sighed. She didn't bother to read it. She would look at it later. One stressful situation at a time.

"That must have been very difficult to deal with," Maria conceded, her heart going out to Terri. She couldn't imagine what it must be like to live with the knowledge that you had killed the man that you loved.

Terri listened as Maria continued, telling her how she had met Anthony and admitting that though they had not been in a real relationship, she had fallen in love with him and he had saved her life. Maria told an engrossing tale, not sparing any details. Terri was riveted. When she was through, she dried her eyes and fished a cigarette from her bag.

"Hope you don't mind but I really need one right now," Maria said as she lit it and took a deep drag.

"No that's fine," Terri said, looking at Maria with a new found respect. She had been through a lot but she had survived, and was now happy. Terri didn't know if they would ever be real friends but she felt no ill will towards her. She now felt a lot better about the situation. At the very least, the brothers would be able to get to know each other.

"Come by the house on Saturday," Terri told her. "We'll formally introduce the kids and let them spend some time with each other. Then we'll take it from there."

Maria nodded.

"Thanks, I'll do that."

They then spent the next half an hour talking about each other's child.

It was amazing.

The brothers were so much alike.

By the time the rain started to drizzle a few minutes later, they were like old friends, giggling like school girls as they jogged to their vehicles.

CHAPTER 18

Anna, Terri's best friend, waited impatiently for her husband to leave the house so that she could check her email. She badly wanted to see Terri's response to her message. She watched as he ate his dinner, noisily chomping his food as he bored her with the details of his day. She attempted to look interested. Anything less would result in an ass whipping right there on the spot. She had been married to him for a year now and it had not taken long for him to show his true colours.

They met in Miami two and a half years ago. Two years after she had awakened from her three month long coma. Fortunately, she had remembered everything and everyone when she woke up. Unfortunately, she had also remembered with extreme clarity, every single detail about her brutal rape and vicious beating at the hands of the *Wolf Man*. It had taken a full year of therapy, and the love and support of Terri and her parents, for her to almost begin feeling human again. Her lifestyle had changed drastically. At the time of the attack, she had been one of Jamaica's top international models, but after she recovered, she no longer had an interest in modeling.

She also lost interest in men and had stayed away from anything with a dick until she met William Carter, the attractive and relatively young Pastor of a small Baptist church in Jacksonville, Florida, in the departure lounge at the Miami International Airport. He had sat beside her and introduced himself and for reasons unknown to her, she conversed with him and had thoroughly enjoyed the twenty minute conversation. Maybe it had been his soft eyes, or his charisma, or his deep but gentle voice, or his aura of wisdom and inherent goodness, but something had clicked, and she had found herself wanting to get to know him better.

He had been a thirty-one year old widower at the time, his wife having died in a car accident just three years into their marriage. They did not have any kids. A one year courtship ensued and Anna got baptized and turned herself over to the Lord; and fourteen months after meeting him in the airport, and despite Terri's dislike of Carter, got married and migrated to Florida.

It was as though she had married the devil himself.

Her honeymoon night, which should have been one of the happiest times of her life, was a nightmare. He had transformed into the devil incarnate when they got to their hotel suite after the brief but sweet ceremony. She had watched in shock, as if it was happening to another person, as the gentle, loving man that had helped her to overcome her fear of men, fucked her like she was a prostitute, not a high class call girl, but like a crack head that was not worth his time but had caught him in the right place at the right time. He had called her every derogatory name in the book as he pummeled her with his dick and fists, continuing to beat her long after he had climaxed.

And that was only the beginning. When they went home, the situation got worse. Her husband, the good Pastor, made her a prisoner in her own home. The phone was kept under lock and key unless he was home, and she was not allowed to have a mobile. She was not allowed to leave home without permission and she was not allowed to have any friends except for the hypocritical women in the church. She was certain that he was sleeping with several of them. The only time she could speak to anyone on the phone, including Terri and her parents, was when he was home as well, sitting right beside her on the couch where he could hear everything.

She had endured the emotional and physical abuse for an entire year, too ashamed to tell Terri or anyone else what she was going through. Terri had *known* that something was wrong when Anna told her it wasn't a good time to visit on both occasions when she was in Florida in the past year, but she hadn't pushed it when Anna kept insisting that she was fine. But during a particularly brutal beating one Monday night after a crusade, while her husband whipped her as he quoted Bible verses and commanded the demons that made his wife a whore and an evil woman to leave her in the name of God, Anna decided that she couldn't take it anymore. She had always been tall and thin, especially during her days as a top model, but now she was downright skeletal. She was scared to death when she looked at herself critically in the mirror that night. She had not recognized the emaciated, hollow-eyed, lifeless creature that stared back at her.

She had to do something.

And soon.

Or she would die.

Though at this juncture that was a welcoming thought.

No more pain.

The thought was appealing.

After what she had gone through with the *Wolf Man*, and to now be going through hell again after giving her life to God, and marrying the man she loved, a man of the cloth no less, it had made her lose faith in life. And God. She wasn't sure what she believed anymore. But after some soul searching, her survival instincts finally kicked in. She didn't survive one of the most brutal attacks that anyone could ever endure and being in a coma for three months so that she could suffer at the hands of a wolf in holy clothing.

She was going to try and get out. She had waited long enough. By now he thought she was broken, fully bended to his demented will. She would show him. She had sent Terri an email just before he got home, having finally figured out the password to the computer. She had not been able to use it without him being present as he didn't give her the password and she was not allowed to have her own computer. But determined, she had sat in front of the computer for an hour, watching the cursor blink in the space where she was supposed to type in the password, when it suddenly came to her. She had typed it in and lo and behold, it worked.

The password was *whore*. His favourite name to call her. The sick bastard.

Without getting into details she had simply told Terri to buy a ticket and book a flight for her to come to Jamaica as soon as possible. And to only respond by email. Knowing Terri, she would do exactly what was requested and ask questions later.

"Are you ok?" he asked, his eyes narrowing suspiciously. "Something seems off about you tonight."

Anna merely looked at him. *Maybe because for the first time since I got married to your psychotic ass I feel alive...I finally have something to look forward to. You sick fuck. I want to take that fork from out of your hand and stab you repeatedly in the face until you scream and beg me to stop hurting you like you have made me do so many times.*

She shrugged and continued to look at him.

The knife in his right hand suddenly connected with her forehead.

Anna squealed.

"I asked you a question woman!" he thundered, looking at her menacingly.

Oh God, why can't he just go and fuck whichever member of his congregation that he has lined up tonight and leave me alone? She mused miserably, rubbing her forehead which was already sporting a small lump. It was Thursday night and he always went back out immediately after dinner on a Thursday, Saturday and Monday. He didn't even bother to clean himself when he came home from fornicating before getting into bed with her. Sometimes he would even force her to suck his dirty miniature dick, and beat her when she gagged from the smell of sex that permeated his genitals.

"I'm sorry William," she said quickly, trying not to antagonize him further. "I'm just not feeling too well. My head hurts."

He grunted and told her to fetch him another knife. She did so and he resumed eating and chatting, as though nothing had happened.

CHAPTER 19

Terri frowned as she read Anna's email. She was sitting in her SUV with the engine idling. Maria had already driven out and the rain was now pouring heavily. Anna was in trouble. Of that she was certain. So many things were off since she had gotten married to that Pastor. Terri had not liked him the moment she met him two years ago. Something about him had given her the creeps. She had not seen her best friend since the wedding and whenever she called, the phone usually rang without an answer and when she did manage to get Anna, she usually sounded strained and sad. And she never called, though her excuse was that her husband didn't like her to make long distance phone calls. Then there was the matter of her not having a cell phone. *I don't need one anymore,* Anna had said, when she brought it up. She was also never online and Anna used to be an internet junkie.

Now she wanted to come home. Whatever was going on, she had decided that she had had enough. Obviously this was something that she was doing behind her husband's back. That spoke volumes. Terri could feel her anger rising. What was that bastard doing to her? She scrolled through her phonebook and called Amoy Kennedy, a friend of hers that owned the travel agency that she usually used. Amoy was home and Terri apologized for bothering her outside of working hours before telling her what she needed. Amoy promised to deal with it for her as soon as possible. Terri thanked her and hung up the phone. She issued a silent prayer to God, asking him to take care of Anna until she got home. She then sent Anna a quick email. The torrent of rain stopped as suddenly as it had begun. Terri was about to drive off when she noticed someone familiar exit a car and walk towards the entrance to the shops. Terri got out and followed.

⚜️❧⚜️❧⚜️❧⚜️

"I am not meeting with anyone!" Noel Steele, the Prime Minister of Jamaica asserted. His personal assistant, Rebecca Smith, looked at him with arched eyebrows. They were in his office going over a few items when he had received the call from *Understanding*.

"I'm the fucking Prime Minister! Do you really expect me to be interrogated about a murder case? You created this problem. You fix it."

Understanding bristled. He did not like anyone shouting at him, especially *God*, who couldn't cut his way out of a wet paper bag. He was the most spineless individual in The Circle. Even *Born*, the lone female, had more balls than he did. But he had his usefulness, and had played his part in helping The Circle to make a lot of money. He was a brilliant orator and all being well, would be Prime Minister for a very long time. At forty-nine, he was the youngest Prime Minister ever, and it wasn't far fetched that he could be in power for three straight terms. With The Circle behind him, anything was possible.

"Save the tantrum," *Understanding* told him impatiently. "I don't have time to waste. You *will* meet with her. It's the only way to deal with it. There's nothing to fear. Just be cool and answer her questions. The only thing she knows is that the number was assigned to your personal assistant. That's it. So I'll let her know that she has an appointment with you tomorrow at 1. I'll speak with you after you have met with her."

Steele terminated the call and threw the phone down onto his desk.

"What's wrong?" Rebecca asked, coming over to rub his shoulders.

"I have to meet with Terri Miller tomorrow," he replied, closing his eyes as her knowledgeable hands massaged his shoulders.

"Don't worry about it," she said soothingly. "You are untouchable. Your code name is *God* for a reason."

Steele flashed his trademark smile that had tricked many voters in the last general election. Rebecca always knew how to stroke his ego, among other things, just right. She had been his personal assistant for three years now. Young, intelligent and striking, she had proven to be invaluable. She knew what she wanted out of life and she knew that he could help her to achieve it. In return, he received unwavering loyalty, someone he could depend on at all times and the best sex he had ever experienced in his life with the exception of the slain prostitute.

His mobile rang. She picked it up and looked at the caller ID.

"It's Mrs. Steele."

The Prime Minister sucked his teeth.

"Tell her I'm in a meeting and cannot be disturbed," he said, waving his hand dismissively.

"Hello, Rebecca Smith speaking," Rebecca said.

Mrs. Steele rolled her eyes when she heard Rebecca's voice. She hated her husband's personal assistant. She just knew that the girl was an opportunist; an educated whore who was probably screwing her husband every chance she got. But she couldn't voice her concerns to Noel. He was a changed man. She couldn't pinpoint exactly when the transformation had begun, but he was longer the loving family man that she had married twenty years ago. He was consumed with power and acted like everyone, including his wife, was beneath him. She would give up all the perks and the status of being the wife of the Prime Minister in exchange for being in a happy and loving marriage. She still loved him tremendously, and was very proud of him, but he had lost his way.

"This is Mrs. Steele, I need to speak with my husband," she said.

Rebecca chuckled inwardly. She could hear the coldness in the woman's voice. Mrs. Steele probably suspected that she was assisting her husband with much more than organizing his day. Tough luck. She had better get used to it. Rebecca wasn't going anywhere anytime soon.

"Mrs. Steele how are you? The Prime Minister is in a meeting right now and unfortunately he cannot be disturbed. Would you like to leave a message?" Rebecca asked sweetly.

"Tell him I need to speak with him urgently."

"Will –" Rebecca stopped in midsentence when she realized that Mrs. Steele had hung up.

She placed the phone back down on the desk.

"She said she needs to speak with you urgently," she said to the Prime Minister as she went over to the office door and locked it.

"Does she now," he whispered hoarsely, knowing what was coming next.

Rebecca walked back over to the desk smiling devilishly. She pushed his chair back and shoving aside the set of files that were in front of him, sat on the edge of the desk and kicked off her heels. She lifted her pleated skirt and spread her legs wide. With his political mentor staring down at him from a portrait on the wall, Noel Steele ripped a hole in the crotch of her stockings, just the way she liked it, and attacked her vagina with his thick lips and anxious tongue. When she moaned 'Oh God', he knew that she wasn't calling on the God above.

<hr/>

Terri watched as the person went inside the ice cream parlour. She waited outside by one of the trees in the rectangular lawn that was surrounded by all the different shops, most of which were now closed at this time of the evening. Only the ice cream parlour and the restaurant were still open. She watched as a young woman, presumably the mother of the little boy that she was glaring at, slapped him for getting ice cream all over his shirt. Terri shook her head sadly. Normally she would have said something to the young woman but she didn't want to be distracted. The little boy cried as his mother pulled him roughly behind her while she headed towards the exit.

Eight minutes passed before Terri's quarry exited the parlour with a white plastic bag holding a container of ice cream. Terri moved quickly, catching up with the person just as she was about to go through the second exit. Terri held her by the elbow and forcefully turned her towards the walk way.

"Come with me," she instructed, her tone and hard grip on the woman's elbow leaving no room for discussion.

The young woman, startled by Terri's sudden appearance, went along with no resistance. They stopped about fifty meters from the exit. Terri looked around. People were close by but not close enough to overhear their conversation.

"What was it that you wanted to talk to me about?" Terri asked, looking her directly in the eyes.

Brenda Bovell, the Police Commissioner's personal assistant, sighed in resignation. She was scared but she was also relieved. She wanted to tell someone what had been happening to her since she started working as the Commissioner's assistant, but she was afraid. His words echoed in her head every time she worked up the nerve to do it, effectively silencing her.

Don't ever speak of this. Your life, and that of your entire family, including your little brother, depends on your co-operation.

She had come very close that day when she followed Terri out to the parking lot at Police Headquarters, but he had called her mobile asking why she wasn't at her desk and that had been that.

Brenda exhaled, and looked away. Tears ran down her sculpted cheeks.

"Let's go sit over there," she said softly, pointing to an empty bench underneath a lignum vitae tree several yards away.

"I bought ice cream for my little brother," she explained, trying to contain her nervousness and fear. "He loves chocolate ice cream."

Terri nodded, smiling tightly. This was a very troubled young woman. Whatever it was that was going on with her was taking a serious toll. The luggage underneath her large, soulful yet extremely sad eyes, told of too many sleepless nights. Terri held on to her elbow, gently this time, and they made their way over to the bench.

"I don't know where to begin," she said in a tiny voice as they sat down on the wooden bench. The previous tenants had eaten chicken and chips. The remnants of their meal were on the ground in front of the bench.

Terri looked away in disgust. A trash can was mere meters away but apparently it would have been too much trouble for them to dispose of their garbage in a civilized manner.

"How about the beginning," Terri suggested with a smile, patting Brenda's hands, which were clutching the bag on her lap tightly.

Her attractive features etched in fear, she looked around before responding.

"It's ok, I can protect you from whatever," Terri told her softly.

Brenda shook her head ruefully.

"I doubt anyone can. Even you," she replied.

She took a deep breath and looked at Terri.

"It's the Commissioner," she began in a voice so soft and low that Terri had to lean in closer. She could faintly smell Brenda's perfume, its scent weakened by a long work day. "H-h-h-he has been raping me at least three times a week since I've started working there."

Terri's jaw dropped. She didn't know what she had expected to hear; maybe that the young woman had witnessed something disturbing or illegal, but not this.

Sweet Jesus.

Brenda started to cry as she continued.

"He just calls me in and has sex with me anytime he wants...makes me suck his...oh God...it's so awful...and degrading...he ejaculates in my mouth... threatened to kill my family if I didn't cooperate...my little brother!"

She doubled over in pain like something had actually happened to her brother.

Terri placed an arm around her.

"I-I-I don't know what I'd do if something happened to Ricky," she sniffed. "Our mom died when he was only three years old...I'm more like his mother than his sister."

"No harm will come to you or your family. That's a *promise*," Terri told her.

It took Brenda several minutes to calm down enough to continue. Terri had a plan. It would require Brenda having to endure more humiliation at the hands of the Commissioner but she agreed to do it. At least this time, it would have a purpose other than the bastard quenching his sexual thirst.

By the time they finished talking, the ice cream had melted.

CHAPTER 20

"I want one to be placed behind him and another facing his desk," Terri instructed. She was in the Police Commissioner's office with Detective Corporal Foster and David, the resident technician expert. At this point, they were the only two people in the Jamaica Police Force that Terri could trust. It was 1 a.m. in the morning. Though she had made her decision over four hours ago to place cameras in the Commissioner's office and had called Foster and David to solicit their assistance, she had waited until such a late hour as she had to be absolutely sure that the entire floor was empty before carrying out her plan.

They were putting their careers on the line to help her out with this one. If they were caught, they would all be in big trouble. Foster didn't care; he was outraged that the Police Commissioner was a rapist and murderer, and would do anything within his power to help bring him down. David was extremely scared and nervous. He was in way over his head but he knew that Terri needed his help so he had reluctantly agreed. He couldn't wait to get it over with and get back into his warm bed. He kept imagining members of the Elite Crimes Unit barging in with guns drawn and arresting all of them.

David quickly installed the tiny but powerful wireless camera high up on the wall above the large window behind the Police Commissioner's desk and then with Foster's assistance, moved the ladder to the opposite side of the room and installed another camera on the wall facing the desk. The cameras were state of the art, a gift from the European Union after an official visit by Terri to Germany six months ago to source new intelligence crime fighting weapons. They would be difficult to spot at a casual glance on the wall as they were see-through with a non-reflective glass eye.

"Ok all done," he said nervously. "I've set a timer on them to begin recording at 8 a.m. to 12 p.m. Any thing that happens inside this office during that time over the next three days will be recorded."

"Thank you so much David," Terri told him. "I owe you one."

"You're welcome Terri," he replied, blushing furiously. Like most men, he had a huge crush on Terri but would never dream of even making a pass at her. "Can we go now?"

Terri and Foster chuckled. They knew that this was probably the most dangerous thing that David had ever done in his life. He was a brilliant technician and his comfort zone was being inside his lab dealing with computers and other electronic gadgets. It was widely believed that he was a virgin and he was the brunt of many jokes around Police Headquarters.

"Ok guys, let's go," Terri said, holding the door open so that they could exit with the ladder. She then looked around the office carefully to ensure that they didn't leave anything askew. Satisfied, she closed the door and left. After learning the things that had taken place in there, being in the Commissioner's office made her skin crawl. Foster and David took the stairs while Terri took the elevator. There were cops on duty on some of the lower floors. It wouldn't be wise for the three of them to be seen together at this hour. The Police Commissioner had eyes everywhere. He might find that suspicious and Terri wasn't ready for him to know that she was on to him.

She was looking forward to confronting him when the time came to throw down the gauntlet. He had let her down in no short order, both on a personal and professional level. Corruption usually started at the top of any organization and filtered down through the ranks. With the police force being one of the most corrupt entities in Jamaica, she should not be fully surprised about the Commissioner. But she was. It was a shocking and disturbing revelation. She had not seen any of this coming. Especially the fact that he was a rapist. Now she knew why he changed assistants so often. Terri sighed and drove out of the parking lot. She turned onto Holborn Road and headed home.

The Police Commissioner would pay dearly for his transgressions.

And soon.

If he thought that he was above the law he had another thing coming.

✵✵✵✵✵✵✵

Anna was too excited to sleep so she was still awake when her husband returned home at 2 a.m. Fortunately, he seemed to have had enough for the night so he ignored her and went straight to sleep. Terri had sent her a quick email. It was the most beautiful two sentences she had ever read.

Hang tight. I'll send you the details soon.

She would be going home soon! She knew where he had hidden her passport. It was in the bottom drawer of the desk in the spare room that doubled as his office. One night when she bought him his meal, he was looking for something in the drawer and she had glimpsed it. The key to the drawer was among the bunch of keys that he always carried with him.

She watched him closely in the semi darkness for several minutes before cautiously getting up and going out into the dining room. He always left the bunch of keys on the hook on the wall. It wasn't there. She didn't want to turn on any lights as the bedroom door was still open and if he woke up and caught her out there without a reasonable explanation, there would be hell to pay.

She maneuvered carefully through the dark house and checked the coffee table. It was there, right on top of the stack of issues of Time Magazine and PC World. She thanked God silently and went into the office. She was so nervous that she dropped the keys when she attempted to open the drawer. Her heart was on her tongue as she froze in fright, praying that he hadn't heard the clang of metal on the floor. Ten agonizingly long seconds ticked by before she exhaled and picked up the keys. She opened the drawer and removed her passport, which was underneath a diary, two bank books and a cheque book. She locked the drawer and returned the keys where she had found them. She then hid the passport in the kitchen. He never went inside the kitchen. Whatever he wanted in there, he always sent her to fetch it.

Her heart beat didn't return to its normal pace until she was back in bed. He had not stirred. He was in the same position that she had left him. She turned her back to him and curled up in the fetal position.

She fell asleep with a smile on her face for the first time in over a year.

CHAPTER 21

"**B**ye Mom," Marc-Anthony said as he kissed his mother on the cheek and hopped out of the vehicle.

"Have a great day honey," Terri told him as she watched him walk towards the understated brick building that was Norfolk Manor, the most exclusive preparatory school in the Caribbean. She had told him that his brother would be coming to visit tomorrow. He tried to act cool about it, yet another trait of his dad, but she knew that he was excited.

Her mobile rang as she headed down Waterworks Road. She glanced at the caller ID. It was the Police Commissioner. Terri kept her emotions in check and answered the phone.

"Good morning, Sir."

"Good morning Terri. I've spoken to the Prime Minister. You will meet with him at 1 p.m. this afternoon."

Terri was surprised. She had actually expected him to give her the runaround. But when she really thought about it, it was a smart move on his part. Arrange a quick meeting to show that there was nothing to hide, find a way to explain the connection regarding the phone number and that would be that.

Or so they thought.

"Ok, that's great," Terri replied.

"I expect a report on my desk this evening," he told her.

"Ok, Sir."

Terri threw the phone on top of her open handbag on the passenger seat. Erwin Baxter had been the Police Commissioner for eleven years. She wondered how long it had taken him to decide that his job of being in charge of the protection of the Jamaican people, was not as interesting as using his lofty post to commit rape and murder, and God knows what else for his own personal gain and satisfaction.

Well he had a good run.

But as they say, all good things must come to an end.

⁕⁖⁘⁙⁕⁖⁘⁙⁕

Terri got to the Police Headquarters at 9:30. Mrs. Green followed her inside her office.

"There's a young lady outside to see you," she said to Terri. "She doesn't have an appointment but she says it's extremely urgent. She has been here for over an hour."

Terri booted up her PC and extracted several files from her attaché case.

"Give me five minutes then send her in," Terri replied.

Exactly five minutes later, Mrs. Green returned with Terri's coffee and the young lady. She then excused herself and closed the door quietly.

"Good morning, I'm Angelina Cortez," she said, extending a hand to Terri.

"Good morning, Ms. Cortez," Terri replied, giving her a quick handshake and indicating for her to sit.

"How can I help you?" Terri asked, taking a sip of her extremely black coffee.

"I'm Alexandra Fletcher's best friend," she replied.

Terri was stunned. She buzzed Mrs. Green on the intercom.

"Do not disturb me for anything for at least an hour."

***

Detective Corporal Foster was in the male bathroom on the eleventh floor which housed the office of the Elite Crimes Unit and several senior detectives, when Detective Corporal Jackson and another member of the ECU walked in. Foster watched them through the mirror above the sink as he washed his hands.

"Foster, you're in the wrong bathroom," Jackson commented, smirking as he made eye contact in the mirror. "The female bathroom is next door."

His partner snickered.

Foster did not rise to the bait. He turned off the pipe, yanked a piece of paper towel from the dispenser and dried his hands. He turned to leave and Jackson stepped in front of him, blocking his way.

"You smell like shit Foster. I guess that comes from kissing Terri Miller's ass all day." ⅄

Foster kneed him in the crotch with a quick deft move, and pushed him to the ground. The other guy glared but did not attempt to attack him.

Foster then left the bathroom wordlessly, ignoring Jackson as he shouted that he was going to kill him from his fetal position on the ground.

Not if I kill you first, you dirty criminal, Foster mused as he made his way to his cubicle.

***

"Alexandra and I met in Las Vegas several years ago where we both worked at an upscale gentleman's club. We became inseparable and even when she returned to Jamaica, we remained best friends. I've been here to see her several times and I usually help her out with her wealthy clients, if you know what I mean."

Terri nodded, fully captivated by what she was hearing.

"The last time I came here, which was about three months ago, we had a session with a man who she said was a very important person. Unknown to him, we taped the session. I have it here on a thumb drive."

Terri almost salivated. She uttered a silent thank you to the man above for this unexpected gift. She tried to contain her excitement as Angelina continued.

"About three weeks ago, Alexandra sent me an email with the file attached. She said I should put it up in a safe place and if anything should ever happen to her, I should contact a cop by the name of Terri Miller in Jamaica."

Terri's mobile rang but she didn't even look at it. Angelina continued.

"I was supposed to come and see her today and the plan was for me to spend two weeks. The last time I heard from her was four days ago. The conversation was brief but she sounded really stressed out and afraid, and she said that we would talk when I got here. I've tried calling her several times since then but got no answer and she hasn't responded to any of my emails or text messages. I knew then that something had happened to her."

Angelina dabbed her eyes with a handkerchief that she retrieved from her bag.

"So last night I scoured the internet, checking the Jamaican newspapers online and lo and behold, there was an article about her murder."

Angelina broke down then, shaking mightily as she sobbed loudly. Terri got up and poured a glass of water which she placed on the desk in front of Angelina, and gently touched her on the shoulder.

"I'm going to get the bastards who killed her. It won't bring her back, but justice will be served," Terri told her softly.

"She was like a sister to me," Angelina said mournfully as she blew her nose and attempted to bring herself under control. "Such a sweet and genuine person. I just had to come and do as she asked. I couldn't live with myself if I didn't."

She drank the water thirstily and dried her face. Now somewhat composed, she dug into her bag and handed the thumb drive to Terri.

Terri took it and attached it to her PC. Her heart was pounding so loudly that she was sure Angelina could hear it. This would turn the case on its head and Angelina's timing couldn't have been better. She needed all the ammunition she could get for her meeting with the Prime Minister. Some concrete proof would go a long way in getting him to understand that his ass was really on the line.

She opened the file and the video started to play. The room, which seemed to be a hotel suite, was well lit. A flabby, hairy man and two women were having sex. At first none of the faces were visible as one of the women was straddling the face of the man with her back turned to the camera while the other was between his legs performing fellatio. After a few minutes, they changed positions and Terri could now see all of the faces clearly. She watched as Alexandra used her mouth to place a condom on the Prime Minister's stubby penis while he kissed Angelina passionately.

Alexandra then climbed onto a chair and the Prime Minister, grunting like a wild boar, entered her doggystyle. He stood wide-legged and fucked her slowly while Angelina crouched between his hairy legs and licked his testicles and anus. Both women referred to him as *God* constantly. The girls then switched positions and five minutes later, both knelt at the feet of the Prime Minister as he removed the condom and pumped his dick furiously until their faces were covered with his juices. Laughing contentedly, he then went into the bathroom. The tape stopped.

Terri leaned back in her chair. Wow. She couldn't believe what she had just witnessed. She looked at Angelina.

"When did you arrive in Jamaica?" she asked, as she copied the file onto her hard drive.

"This morning. I came straight to here from the airport. I googled you last night and found out where your office was so I just took a cab straight from the airport. I travelled light. This is my only bag," Angelina told her, blinking back a fresh batch of tears as she gestured to the Luis Vuitton bag on the chair next to her.

"When are you leaving?" Terri asked, taking out the thumb drive and handing it to her.

"No, keep it," Angelina said, shaking her head. "I'm leaving tomorrow morning. I booked a suite at Chateau Grand."

Terri looked at the time. It was now 10:38.

"I'll give you a ride over there," Terri offered. It was the least she could do and besides, she could use some air.

"Thanks, I appreciate it," Angelina said. She took a small Mac kit from her bag and retouched her make-up.

They then exited the office and Mrs. Green watched them curiously as they walked by and waited for the elevator.

"You're a very beautiful woman," Angelina commented on the ride down. "You would make a killing in my profession."

Terri smiled at the backhanded compliment.

"Thanks, I think," she responded.

They both laughed.

After chatting with her some more and exchanging numbers so that they could keep in touch, Terri left Angelina in the hotel lobby and made her way back to Police Headquarters. She was feeling that adrenaline rush that she always felt when she was at a critical juncture in a case. This was a big dirty one, and the fallout from this would be really grave on many levels but she had to press forward. No one, absolutely no one, was above the law.

She had the Prime Minister right where she wanted him.

By his scrawny, wrinkled testicles.

And at 1 p.m. this afternoon, she was going to squeeze.

Hard.

CHAPTER 22

"No, get her on a flight for Sunday instead," Terri said to Amoy, her travel agent friend whom she had asked to take care of Anna's travel details. "Preferably mid morning."

"Ok, I'll call you back later," Amoy told her.

Terri hung up and exited her vehicle. She had just gotten back to Police Headquarters. It was now 11:15. She needed to go and prepare for her meeting with the Prime Minister. She was looking forward to it. By 2 p.m., an hour after the meeting had begun, if everything went according to plan, she would be armed with enough information to put some serious heat on everyone involved in the murder of the prostitute as well as the subsequent killings of the lawyer and the technician. Somebody was going to spend the weekend in jail. These were some powerful people but if she made an arrest late enough this evening, that person would at the very least have to spend the weekend in jail. Who was that person going to be?

Terri couldn't wait to find out.

Terri arrived at Jamaica Royal at 12:50 p.m. Originally built to be the official residence of the Prime Minister of Jamaica, it now mainly housed the Prime Minister's office, and recently, a basic school. Terri showed her credentials to the security personnel at the gate, who though they recognized her, asked for identification. Terri then proceeded along the circular picturesque driveway and parked in the area designated for visitors. Clutching her Prada bag, she confidently strode inside the building after showing her identification to another cop standing at the entrance. Terri then entered the elaborate foyer, and her heels clicked on the highly polished wooden floor as she was shown to the lobby of the Prime Minister's office. There were three receptionists in this area. Two of them looked positively bored.

A waste of taxpayer's money, Terri mused.

At 1:05, one of the receptionists answered her intercom and told Terri that she could go in. Terri thanked her politely and made her way through the large oak door.

The Prime Minister remained seated in the leather swivel chair behind his expansive mahogany desk. Past Prime Ministers stared down from the walls on either side of the room.

"Sit," he said curtly.

Terri did so, smiling inwardly. If he thought for one moment that his rude and abrupt attitude would have an effect on her, he was dead wrong. He was nothing but a choir boy that had gone to the right schools, met the right people and managed to scramble to the top of an uninspiring political heap. She had not voted for him in the last election.

Rebecca Smith, his personal assistant, stood to his left like a watchdog. She stared at Terri with open hostility. Terri ignored her and focused her attention on the bespectacled Prime Minister.

She got straight to the point.

"What is your connection to Alexandra Fletcher, the dead prostitute?"

The Prime Minister frowned. He had expected her to be a bit rattled by the hostile tone that he had set the moment she walked through the door, but she was far from intimidated by him or his office. She had gotten straight to it, matching his unfriendly businesslike attitude. It was his first time meeting her but like every Jamaican over the age of four, he knew a lot about the celebrated cop. The only honest cop in Jamaica, people loved to say. Public opinion was that she was also the most beautiful woman in Jamaica.

He didn't like her but looking at her critically up close, it was difficult to disagree.

"I have no connection to the woman you mentioned," was the curt reply.

"A mobile number, registered to Rebecca Smith, who I gather is your personal assistant, was in the dead woman's contact information," Terri continued without missing a beat. "Why would that be?"

"Perhaps it was an error. People record wrong numbers all the time. Neither Ms. Smith, nor any one associated with this office, knows that woman," he responded dismissively.

Terri decided that she would not waste any more time.

"I see. Then how is it possible that I have in my possession a video of you having sex with Alexandra Fletcher and another woman?" Terri asked nonchalantly.

The Prime Minister could not contain his surprise. His mouth became a wide O.

Then he quickly composed himself. She had to be bluffing. Where the hell could she have gotten that?

"Prove it," he challenged.

Terri removed the thumb drive from her hand bag. Rebecca Smith moved forward and took it from her. The tension in the room could be cut with a knife as she attached it to a sleek Sony Vaio laptop that was on the Prime Minister's desk and opened up the file. The image of a man having sex with two women came on the screen. The Prime Minister's heart tip toed on his tongue. He recognized the room. It was a suite at Hotel Monaco. He remembered that night. It was the night before his birthday. It had been great. And now it was back to bite him in the ass. Who had recorded it? Must have been one of those bitches.

Jesus Christ.

He felt ill.

He watched as Alexandra got up from off his tongue and he sat up, his mouth slick with her juices, his face now fully in view of the camera.

"Turn it off!" he snapped. Rebecca jerked like she was coming out of a trance and stopped the tape.

"Leave us," he instructed hoarsely.

Rebecca looked at him with a pained expression and left the room on heavy legs, her mind churning, wondering what the hell was going to happen now. This was a crisis of astronomical proportions. How would he handle it? She closed the door softly and went inside her office. She rummaged through her Yves Saint Laurent handbag, a gift from the Prime Minister, and extracted a pack of Marlboro Red. She shook a cigarette free and lit it, inhaling deeply. Smoking was not allowed inside the building but right now she didn't give a fuck. She needed to calm her nerves. She wondered what was happening inside the Prime Minister's office. Poor Noel.

Noel Steele slumped in his chair. Gone was the bravado. Gone was the arrogance. Disbelief, fear and helplessness had taken over. He briefly contemplated ripping out the thumb drive and destroying it but that would be useless. There was no doubt that she had copies elsewhere. There was nothing he could do. He was at her mercy. He removed his spectacles and wiped his eyes.

"Just tell me what you want...I'll give you anything to suppress this," he said, finally breaking the prolonged silence.

Terri looked at him for a long moment, her face a stoic mask. Beads of perspiration decorated his prominent forehead despite the air conditioning. He loosened his tie a bit.

"Here's the deal and it's not negotiable. You give me your full cooperation – no lies – and I'll allow you to serve out most of what remains of your term. But you will resign before the next election and you can never hold public office again," Terri told him.

Steele looked up at the photographs of the former Prime Ministers on the wall. He doubted any of them had ever had to deal with a situation like this. He had no choice. If this tape got out he would be forced to resign in disgrace. His wife would divorce him. He would be unwelcome in Jamaican high society. He would become a pariah. Not even The Circle could help him now. So much for unlimited power, as *Understanding* liked to often boast.

His life as he knew it was over. He was planning to call a general election in fourteen months. His party would have won hands down. The opposition was currently in disarray and would be unable to mount a serious campaign. He had so many plans for the country, so many policies that he wanted to enact, to help Jamaica become better equipped to stay afloat in these tough economic times, but it was all over now. He would have to resign within a year. He released a heavy sigh as he nodded sadly.

"Ok, I agree," he said in a voice cracked with emotion.

Terri removed a miniature tape recorder from her handbag and set it on the table. She didn't turn it on. She then took out a small note pad, a 23k trim fountain Parker pen and a sheet of paper. She handed him the paper. It was a copy of the list of numbers with the unique code names.

"I already know that you are *God*, but write down who the others are beside their code names," she instructed.

Steele put back on his glasses and removing a pen from his shirt pocket, began to write.

Terri was feeling great as she watched him scribble nervously. Everything was going according to plan. Steele would do anything to keep her from making the video public. God bless Angelina. She had given her the leverage she needed to tip the scales in her favour. Justice would be served.

He finished and shoved the sheet of paper over to Terri. She picked it up and read it. Erwin Baxter, the

Police Commissioner, and her dear mentor, was *Understanding*. Douglas Fairchild, Governor of the Bank of Jamaica, was *Knowledge*. Lionel Lee, President of the Private Sector Union of Jamaica was *Cipher*. And Terri's initial guess was right. *Born* was indeed a woman. Elizabeth Martin-Cole, the Attorney General of Jamaica. And so the list went. Ten of the most powerful people on the island.

Terri turned on the tape recorder and clasped her hands underneath her chin.

"Identify yourself," she instructed.

"I'm Noel Steele, Prime Minister of Jamaica," he said, in a cracked but audible voice.

"Are you aware that this interview is being recorded?"

"Yes."

"Who killed Alexandra Fletcher?"

"I don't know who actually carried out the murder, probably one of the cops from the Elite Crimes Unit, but it was ordered by Police Commissioner Erwin Baxter."

"And the other murders?"

"He was responsible for those killings as well."

Terri kept her emotions in check as she remembered poor little Gilbert Chen. She continued.

"Why was Fletcher murdered?"

"According to *Understanding*, I mean Baxter, she knew too much and also wanted to stop working for us. He didn't think it was safe to let her go."

"What is the significance of the circle drawn be-side each of the code names?"

"The ten of us are members of a secret society called The Circle."

"Tell me everything about The Circle."

Terri listened intently as he spoke.

She chuckled inwardly.

The son of a bitch even managed to sound nostalgic.

CHAPTER 23

Police Commissioner Erwin Baxter slammed the phone down. He could not get through to the Prime Minister. His personal line rang without an answer twice and when he called the main line, the receptionist had advised him that the Prime Minister was in a meeting and could not be disturbed. And Rebecca Smith was not answering her extension or her mobile. It was now 2:45. Why the hell was he still in a meeting with Terri Miller? For almost two hours? Something wasn't right. He had a very bad feeling about this. He was no longer in control of the situation and that was not good. He paced the room before stopping by the mini bar to pour a shot of Johnny Walker Black Label. He downed it in one gulp.

He regretted allowing the meeting to take place. At the very least he should have been there as well.

But how was he supposed to know that Terri would have had the Prime Minister hemmed up in his office for close to two hours? Terri Miller was too smart and resourceful for her own good. She obviously had something up her sleeve. Maybe she had kept something from him in the report. He could feel a headache coming on. He opened his top desk drawer and removed a vial of cocaine. He emptied it on his desk and using a small ruler, made a neat line. He then rolled a crisp thousand dollar bill and snorted the entire line up his right nostril. It had an instant calming effect.

He was now feeling like his old invincible self. No use wasting time wondering what was going on at the Prime Minister's office. It was time to act. He picked up the phone and called Detective Corporal Jackson and issued instructions. He then buzzed Brenda, his personal assistant.

A quickie was in order.

***

Elizabeth Martin-Cole, the Attorney General of Jamaica, thought for a moment before responding. She was shell-shocked. The Prime Minister had just called her, and put her on the phone with Police Superintendent Terri Miller. What the Superintendent had to say had almost given her a heart attack. This was not supposed to be happening. And it was all

Understanding's fault. If he hadn't gotten so caught up with that high class hooker this would never have happened. But he had, and now the dead whore's ghost, and those of the other people that he had ordered to be killed, were back to haunt them.

Revenge from the grave.

And now she was caught up in the mix. She could not afford to be arrested as an accessory to murder, as the Superintendent had threatened, if she didn't cooperate. At this point, she had no choice. She doubted that she would be actually convicted but that wasn't the point. The damage would have already been done. She would have to resign and the integrity of one of the highest offices in the land would be compromised. Steele had already panicked and sold them out, hoping to save his own skin.

Fucking wimp, she mused contemptuously. She was already thinking ahead. All the Superintendent wanted was someone to pay the price for the three murders. If they all cooperated and handed over *Understanding* as the sacrificial lamb, then all would not be lost. The Superintendent had enough evidence for a conviction. The Police Commissioner and his hit squad, also known as the Elite Crimes Unit, were going down.

The Circle would regroup and go on.

With a new, less unpredictable, more civilized leader.

Her.

"I'll sign the warrant for his arrest," she agreed.

"Ok, Detective Corporal Foster will be coming to see you within forty-five minutes. Ensure its ready when he gets there," Terri instructed, adding, "and don't be late for the meeting at Police Headquarters on Monday morning 9 a.m. sharp."

Elizabeth Martin-Cole hung up without responding. The Superintendent had ordered her to round up the members of The Circle for a meeting in her office on Monday morning. *Everyone* had to be there. She sighed and got out her cell phone. Damn *Understanding* for putting them in this predicament.

He was going to get exactly what he deserved.

He made his bed and now he had to lie in it.

�֎֎֎֎֎֎

Brenda grimaced, her attractive face a mask of pain and hatred as she gripped the edge of the desk tightly. The Police Commissioner was behind her, all 6'4", 250 lbs of him, pummeling away. As usual, she was arid and he was huge and rough. Not a good combination. She took solace in the fact that this was the last time that she would be going through this. Superintendent Miller had promised and she believed her. The Police Commissioner's weekly sexual assaults had made her a changed woman. She had left her loving boyfriend and the look on his face when she told him that it was over without any explanation had cut her deeply. But how could she have told him? And the shame and helplessness she felt about the situation had robbed her of her happiness. She was now a shadow of her former self. Withdrawn and surly, and perpetually filled with suicidal thoughts, only Ricky, her little brother, had prevented her from taking her own life.

She couldn't do that to him.

He needed her.

Hopefully, one day, when this was over, she would be able to recover from her mental and physical scars, and move on with her life.

The air conditioning hummed loudly.

She groaned louder as his pace picked up considerably.

The pain was almost unbearable but the end was near.

Thankfully, he was about to climax.

She clenched her teeth together in a mighty effort to prevent from screaming as he plundered her insides, embracing his orgasm.

He shuddered and grunted, and was done.

He sat in his chair, the condom still on his almost flaccid member jutting from his fly, and she pulled up her underwear, pulled down her skirt, and went inside his bathroom to get a rag to clean him up.

Terri returned Amoy's call as she walked out to the parking lot. Her job here was done. She had left the Prime Minister in his office looking like the world had come to an end. Well it had. For him anyway. Foster was on his way to the Attorney General's office to pick up the warrant for the arrest of the Police Commissioner for three counts of first degree murder. There would be more arrests – members of the Elite Crimes Unit, but that would come later. She had instructed the Prime Minister not to speak to the Police Commissioner under any circumstances. Terri had no doubt that he was probably trying to reach the Prime Minister and was getting concerned that he was unable to make contact. She wanted to get to him before he left Police Headquarters. That was where she wanted to arrest him and march him downstairs instead of taking the elevator so everyone on each floor could see him in handcuffs. He deserved the embarrassment. She had also instructed Foster to put together a team of eight cops to escort them to the Half-Way-Tree police station where the Commissioner would be booked and held. They were assembled at Police Headquarters in two vehicles in the parking lot awaiting her arrival. They had no idea what was going on.

"Sorry I missed your calls," Terri apologized. "I was in a very important meeting."

"No problem Terri...I know how it goes sometimes. I got her on a 1 p.m. flight on Sunday. That was the best I could do," Amoy told her.

"That's perfect," Terri replied. "Email me the ticket. And thanks a million Amoy. We'll do lunch next week."

"I won't hold my breath," Amoy joked. They both knew that Terri was busy most of the time and it could be awhile before they actually hooked up for lunch. "You're welcome. Talk soon."

Terri laughed.

"Bye Amoy, catch you later."

She couldn't wait to see Anna. But first things first. She was about to cause a stir island wide. When word of the Police Commissioner's arrest hit the media and the streets, there was going to be pandemonium.

CHAPTER 24

Terri switched over to the left lane and stopped on red at the light. The passenger window of the vehicle next to her, a black Mitsubishi Pajero, came down as they beeped the horn to get her attention.

She looked over but kept her window up as a familiar face that she couldn't quite place stuck his head out and said something to her. She cautiously put the window down halfway to hear what he was saying.

"Are you Superintendent Miller?" the man asked.

Terri looked inside the vehicle, the driver was wearing a cap and wrap around sunglasses and was staring straight ahead but his profile looked familiar.

She recognized him just as she was showered with glass. Someone had smashed the passenger window on her SUV. Terri screamed and pulled her gun as she sped off, barely missing the last vehicle that had turned right coming from the opposite direction just as the light changed to green. The man with the metal bat hopped into the black Montero Sport that was behind her and gave chase along with the black Mitsubishi Pajero. The three SUVs weaved dangerously through traffic as Terri raced towards Police Headquarters.

She was shaken but not afraid. They were members of the Elite Crimes Unit. Detective Corporal Jackson was driving the vehicle that had pulled up beside her at the stoplight. They had to be acting on the Police Commissioner's orders. They didn't want to kill her or she would have been dead already. They wanted to kidnap her. She ran the red light at the intersection of Trafalgar Road and Knutsford Boulevard and her pursuers did likewise, the Pajero slamming into a Honda Fit, brushing it aside before continuing on in pursuit.

With her firearm in her lap, Terri suddenly turned left, then veered right, then left again, dropping out on Trinidad Terrace. She skillfully maneuvered the vehicle as she reached for her mobile and called Foster. Good thing she had him on speed dial.

"Foster!" Terri said, as she skipped around a line of traffic and made an illegal right turn onto Oxford Road, causing a three car collision. "I was attacked by the ECU. I'm on my way to Police Headquarters and they are chasing me."

"What! Are you ok? Shit!" Foster exclaimed. He

couldn't believe that they would dare attack the Superintendent. "I just got the warrant and I'm leaving now to meet you down there."

"I'm fine, see you in a bit."

Terri could see one of the vehicles still behind her a few cars back. The Mitsubishi Pajero driven by Jackson. Adrenaline pumped as she neared Police Headquarters. She wondered what they planned to do when she finally stopped. Well she would find out soon enough.

⁂

Detective Corporal Jackson ignored the constant vibration of the mobile on his waist as he tried vainly to catch up with Terri Miller. He knew that it was the Police Commissioner calling and he would be pissed when he learnt that Terri Miller had gotten away. The plan had been to snatch her at the stoplight but the bitch had reacted quickly, catching them off guard. He *had* to catch her. She was heading to Police Headquarters. Randy, who was driving the Montero Sport, was nowhere to be seen. He hoped that he had smartly surmised that was where the Superintendent was heading and was there waiting to cut her off.

He temporarily lost sight of her Mercedes SUV as it zipped around the corner onto Dominica Drive. He turned the corner just in time, narrowly escaping hitting a Volvo sedan driven by a pregnant woman, who also had her four year old son travelling with her, just in time to see Terri's SUV make a beeline for the parking lot of Police Headquarters. He stepped on it and entered the parking lot, his tyres screeching loudly as he came to an abrupt stop, desperate to catch her before she entered the building.

He didn't have to worry about that.

She was standing by her vehicle waiting for him.

CHAPTER 25

Terri watched calmly as the three men exited the vehicle quickly, slowing down uncertainly when they realized that she was just standing there, waiting for them.

"Why she not running?" the one everyone called Hulk because of his bulky, muscular physique asked.

Jackson pulled his firearm and walked towards Terri, his face in a tight scowl.

"Just knock her unconscious and throw her in the truck," he responded, ignoring Hulk's question. He had no idea why she was just standing there like she was safe but he had orders to carry out and by God he would. His ass was on the line.

When they got about forty meters to Terri, the eight policemen that were awaiting Terri's instructions circled the three men from behind, training their weapons on them.

"Stop! Put your guns down and put your hands in the air!" Terri instructed, raising her own weapon and pointing it Jackson.

The men stopped. The other two turned around and pointed their guns at the group of cops approaching them warily but steadily, whilst Jackson kept his attention on Terri.

He grinned.

"Seems like we have a Mexican standoff, Superintendent Miller," he said, still grinning.

"Jackson! Put down your gun!" Foster, who had just arrived and joined the fray shouted as he walked up to them, his gun trained on the back of Jackson's head. "Don't dig a deeper hole for yourself than the one you're already in. Put down your weapon and get on the ground!"

Jackson turned his head to look at Foster, a man he disliked so much that he had mentally killed him a thousand different ways every time he laid eyes on him.

"Well well...if it isn't the biggest ass kisser in the Police Force. Fuck you Foster. Come and take my gun from me," he challenged, just before a bullet shattered his right wrist, turning it into a mass of bleeding distorted flesh, and eliciting a piercing high pitched scream which seemed to have travelled all the way from his toes. His gun went off when it hit the concrete, the bullet lodging itself into Hulk's groin.

Hulk looked down in disbelief at his crotch before falling to his knees. The remaining cop that was with Jackson slowly knelt and placed his gun on the ground whilst yelling 'Don't shoot!'

"Four of you get the wounded two to the hospital and place them under police guard," Terri instructed, putting her gun back inside the holster, watching as Foster slapped a pair of handcuffs on the one that was lying on the ground. Foster hauled him up and placed him in the back of an unmarked police car and locked the doors.

"The rest of you follow me," Terri said after Foster handed her the warrant for the arrest of the Police Commissioner.

It was time for the main event.

CHAPTER 26

Police Headquarters was in a state of disarray. Someone had gotten a glimpse of what was happening in the parking lot through a window on the fourth floor and had raced back to his department to tell the others. Cops were shooting it out with cops in the parking lot! By the time Terri, her face cut and bleeding, with tiny shards of glass still all over her clothes and in her hair, made her way purposefully inside with Foster and the four other cops behind her, no one inside was working. Everyone watched with a thousand questions on their shocked faces as the group of six got into an elevator and went up to the twelfth floor.

Police Commissioner Erwin Baxter was furious. What the fuck was wrong with everyone? He still wasn't getting through to the Prime Minister or any member of The Circle for that matter. He had just called *Born's* mobile but it rang without an answer. The mobile phones of three other members, *Knowledge*, *Cipher* and *Wisdom* were off and they were not at their offices. And now he had called Detective Corporal Jackson three times and his phone just rang out to voicemail. He needed to calm down before he popped a blood vessel. He opened his drawer to sniff a line of cocaine but there was none. He slammed the drawer shut and grabbed his keys. He felt like his anger and frustration was about to suffocate him. He wasn't used to not being in control. He needed some air. Heads were going to roll tonight. That much he could promise everyone. He was heading towards the door when it flew open without warning.

Terri Miller, accompanied by Foster and four other policemen, entered his office.

She looked at him for a moment. Her face wore a stoic expression. She was silent but her eyes spoke loudly, telling the story of the many emotions that she was feeling.

Disappointment. Resentment. Anger. Conviction. Victory.

The Police Commissioner went on the offensive.

"What is the meaning of this?" he thundered authoritatively. "Speak up Miller!"

"You are under arrest for ordering the murders of Alexandra Fletcher, Martin Meyers and Gilbert Chen," Terri told him without preamble, handing him the warrant.

He snatched it from her outstretched hand and read the document. He couldn't believe that *Born* would sign a warrant for his arrest. Her signature could only mean one thing. They had sold him out. Now he understood why the Prime Minister's meeting with Terri had taken so long and why he had been unable to get through to anyone since then. Did they really think it was that simple? That he would go quietly to prison in shame and embarrassment while they got away scotch free and continued to flourish and enjoy the fruits of *his* labour? He had created The Circle. He created *them.* They owed everything to him; especially that disloyal back-biting, spineless son of a bitch Steele and that cunt Martin-Cole. They would have never gotten where they were without him. And this was how they repaid him. If they had stuck together they would have made it through this. He would have eventually eradicated this problem and it would have been back to business as usual.

"Are you stupid?" he sneered. "You can't arrest *me.*"

Terri nodded to Foster and he stepped over to the Police Commissioner with a pair of handcuffs.

The Police Commissioner floored him with a vicious right-handed punch that caught him flush on the right cheek.

"Take him down!" Terri instructed. The other four cops grabbed the Commissioner, and after two frenetic minutes, finally pinned him down long enough for Terri to handcuff him.

"Are you ok?" she asked as she went over to check on Foster, who was sitting up on the floor holding his jaw.

She helped him up and examined him.

"It seems fractured," she said, her diagnosis confirmed when he tried unsuccessfully to speak, his eyes watering from the pain.

"Get someone to drive you to the hospital. We'll go on ahead and finish up," Terri told him.

Foster nodded and they hauled the Police Commissioner to his feet. Terri led the way out and it was as though the entire staff at Police Headquarters was now working on the twelfth floor. The place was packed. Terri winked subtly at Brenda, the Police Commissioner's personal assistant, as she walked by. Brenda was smiling with tears in her eyes.

Erwin Baxter was a picture of defiance as they led him to the elevator. If he was embarrassed by what was happening, he hid it well. He glared at everyone as he walked by, his eyes wild and his chest heaving from his scuffle with the cops.

It was a circus when they got downstairs. The media had gotten wind of the situation and were out in their numbers. They were denied entrance to the building by two stone faced cops at the entrance to the lobby but they went wild at the sight of the Police Commissioner in handcuffs. Cameras flashed and questions were shouted as they took the Police Commissioner over to a tinted police van. He went inside it without any resistance, no doubt wanting to get away from the relentless glare of the cameras as quickly as possible.

The lead vehicle, a marked squad car with its siren blaring loudly, headed out and was followed by the van transporting the Police Commissioner and an unmarked police car in which Terri and two cops were travelling. Cars pulled over to the soft shoulder to allow them to pass and they quickly made their way to the Half-Way-Tree police station.

Terri was in a pensive mood. It was a bittersweet victory. She was still trying to reconcile the man that she thought she had known with the animal that was riding in the vehicle in front of her. It was a difficult task.

And it was only the beginning of what was sure to be a long, drawn out high profile process. People of the Police Commissioner's stature rarely went to jail or were held accountable for their actions. But not this time. He could hire as many high priced lawyers as he wished, but the outcome would not change. The evidence was too overwhelming.

They arrived at the Half-Way-Tree police station and the cops there, though they had gotten word that the

Police Commissioner had been arrested for murder, watched in shock as he was indeed led into the station in handcuffs. It was an unbelievable sight.

"Book him," Terri instructed to the Sergeant in charge of the station, without preamble.

"B-b-but shouldn't we discuss this first? Let's go in my office," he said, his beady eyes shifting from Terri to the Police Commissioner and back to Terri again nervously. He was one of the Police Commissioner's die hard men, and had abused the law on several occasions at the Commissioner's behest.

Terri walked up to him until her face was mere inches away from his. She could smell his stale sweat and cheap cologne.

"Are you refusing to do your job Sergeant? Book the prisoner now! There's nothing to discuss!" she commanded, the room deathly quiet as everyone watched the drama unfold.

"Book him rass! After him no betta than mi!" a disheveled man who was in handcuffs on a bench in the corner proclaimed loudly, breaking the silence.

He was treated to a vicious back-handed slap by an officer standing close by.

"Shut yuh mouth!" the officer snarled.

Terri glared at the cop for a moment, the scowl on her face showing her disapproval at his actions, but turned her attention back to the Sergeant.

He reluctantly ordered that the Police Commissioner be fingerprinted and logged into the system as a prisoner.

He apologized profusely to the Commissioner during the entire process. The Police Commissioner merely smiled and told him not to worry about it. He then requested his phone call and was quickly handed a cell phone. He spoke to his lawyer briefly and was then led to an empty cell. There were three holding cells at the police station and the Sergeant in charge had quickly removed all the prisoners from one of the cells and relocated them to the other two so that the Police Commissioner would be in a cell by himself. That meant the other cells were severely crowded and though some of the prisoners cursed, there was nothing they could do about it. Terri didn't approve but the Sergeant insisted that it was for the Police Commissioner's safety.

Terri then left the station and was heading back to Police Headquarters when the Prime Minister rang her mobile.

"I have to do an urgent press conference," he said. "The media is going crazy. I have to give a statement. The Deputy Police Commissioner will be with me and so should you. Come to Jamaica Royal as soon as possible. We'll wait until you get here."

Terri agreed and hung up.

She went back to Police Headquarters to clean up her face and comb her hair, before getting a junior detective to drive her to Police Headquarters. Thankfully the scratches were tiny and barely visible when she covered them with make-up. While on the way she called her Mercedes dealer for them to send a representative to pick up her SUV which was still in the parking lot at Police Headquarters, so that the smashed window could be replaced and the vehicle cleaned up. She had left the keys at the front desk downstairs. She then checked her email and seeing the e-ticket there for Anna's flight, quickly forwarded it to Anna's email address.

She arrived at Jamaica Royal in fifteen minutes and was quickly taken in to the Prime Minister's office. He greeted her much more warmly this time and she shook the hands of the Deputy Police Commissioner who would be now charged with running the police force until a permanent choice was named. Terri got along with him well enough, and though he was a good man, he lacked the kind of steeliness required to head the police force of one of the countries with the highest murder rate in the world.

The Prime Minister showed her his brief statement that he would be giving at the hastily arranged press conference. He would be flanked by Terri and the Deputy Police Commissioner at the podium. Terri nodded her approval and they quickly headed to the conference room where the media was anxiously waiting.

Anna was in seventh heaven. She had just chanced another glance at her email and saw the message from Terri. She glanced worriedly at the clock – her husband could come home any time now, and sent the ticket to print. She chewed off her right nail by the time the document was finished printing. She then moved quickly. She shut the computer down, retrieved the ticket from off the printer, closed the door and made her way to the bedroom. She placed the ticket in the inside pocket of the jacket for the skirt suit that she would be wearing to church tomorrow, where she already had her passport and a hundred and twenty dollars that she had found in one of her husband's pants pocket. She was so nervous that she became afraid that when he got home he would notice that something was amiss. She couldn't afford for that to happen. She *had* to get out of this marriage.

The sound of the powerful engine of her husband's Lincoln Navigator pulling into the driveway made her jump nervously. She quickly closed the closet and went out into the living room, sat on the couch and picked up the Bible. He liked to see her reading it. Her heart raced as she heard his key in the door. She prayed to God that everything would work out. If it did, by tomorrow this time she would be in Jamaica.

CHAPTER 27

Terri got home at 9:00 p.m. She was exhausted. It had been a hell of a day. She had just viewed the tape of the cameras that were placed inside the Police Commissioner's office. It had been difficult to watch. The issue of rape had always been a sore spot with her and after the *Wolf Man* case and what had happened to Anna, there were few things in life that she despised more than a rapist. Poor Brenda. At least it was now over. He would never be able to touch her again. She had not told anyone about the existence of the tape. Only Foster and David, the technician, knew about it. She planned to use it as a surprise bargaining chip to get the Police Commissioner to plead guilty to all charges and spare the State the expense of going to trial.

Marc-Anthony, wearing striped blue pajamas, greeted his mother at the door.

"Hey baby," Terri gushed as she hugged and kissed him.

"Hi Mommy. How was your day?" he asked, holding her hand as she walked to her bedroom.

"Very adventurous." She tossed her laptop on the bed, before plopping down next to it.

"I saw you on the news tonight," he announced, climbing on top of her. "You looked so serious. But you were still pretty."

Terri chuckled. Her son was something else. She had seen the news as well on the T.V. in her office. Naturally, the Police Commissioner's arrest was the biggest news in the country. The country was in shock. It was a double edged sword. There was no doubt that it was a damaging blow and would reinforce the popular perception of just how corrupt the police force was and, for honest cops, it would definitely have an adverse effect on their morale. But on the other hand, the arrest would show that the police force was serious about weeding out corruption within its ranks, even if it was at the very top.

"Thanks honey," Terri said, looking up at her son's handsome face. It was like looking at a pint sized version of his father. Anthony knew what he was doing when he had spilled his seed inside her. He had ensured that she would never forget him. No matter what. But that was okay. She didn't want to forget him. She simply needed to get over him. And Nico was helping in that regard slowly but surely. She couldn't wait to see him. He was due to arrive in Jamaica in a couple of weeks.

Terri sat up and cradled her only child in her arms. He was getting so big. Or tall rather. His father had been six feet tall and with his mother no slouch in the height department – she was 5'10" - he was destined to be a tall young man.

"Looking forward to spending time with your brother tomorrow?" she asked, playing with the mop of unruly curls on his head.

He nodded with a serious smile. Terri wondered if they would get along and would be close as the years went by. She sure hoped so. That would be nice. She got up with a grunt, allowing Marc-Anthony to stand.

"You're getting too heavy for me young man," she teased. "I can't lift you anymore."

Marc-Anthony grinned and flexed his bony triceps in response. Terri laughed heartily as they headed out to the kitchen.

She was starving.

⁂

Mrs. Roper, the former secretary for Martin Meyers, the murdered lawyer, was thoughtful after watching the news at 10. She was in bed with her husband, who was lying next to her on his back like a beached whale, snoring loudly with his mouth slightly open. The Police Commissioner had been charged for the murders of Alexandra Fletcher and her former boss! She wondered if her involvement, however unwilling it had been, would come out in the investigation. She could go to jail as an accessory to murder!

She got out of bed and paced the floor, trying to decide if she should go to the police and explain how she had been forced to spy on her boss and provide information to persons unknown, or if should she just wait it out and see what happened. She made her way to the bathroom. She had a sudden urge to pee. There was a saying that trouble always came in threes. It was so true. First her boss had been murdered and she was now out of a good paying job. She had a big fight with her lover who was not accepting her calls, and after getting used to having good sex with him at least three times a week, she was now horny and ir-ritable all the time. And now, even more serious, there was a possibility that she could get in trouble with the law.

At forty-three she was too old for this shit.

She sighed, wiped, flushed, washed her hands and returned to bed.

She decided to wait it out and keep her fingers crossed.

She was so edgy she almost woke her husband up to give her some but on second thought, five minutes worth of sex wouldn't do her much good right now. She turned the TV off and tried to get some sleep.

CHAPTER 28

"**H**i Terri! So nice to see you again," Maria said, as the two women hugged. She then knelt and pinched Marc-Anthony playfully on the cheek.

"And how are you today Marc-Anthony?" she asked, giving him a warm smile.

"I'm fine," he replied, stealing a quick look at his brother before settling his pretty grey eyes on her once more.

"Well I'm Maria and this Diego, your brother," she said.

The two six year old siblings looked at each other without speaking.

Marc-Anthony broke the ice by asking Diego if he wanted to play video games.

"You can't beat me," Diego challenged as Marc-Anthony led the way to the fluffy cushions on the carpeted floor in front of the Plasma TV on the wall. The adults watched bemused as he smirked, confidently turned on his Xbox and handed Diego a set of controls.

They plopped down on the cushions and it was game on.

Terri wanted to tell them to wait until after breakfast – Mavis was in the process of setting the picnic table out in the small backyard – but she didn't dare interrupt them. Lego Star Wars came on the large screen and the kids went at it, staring at the screen intensely as their little fingers knowledgeably moved around the controls at the speed of light.

"Diego has this game at home too," Maria whispered.

They watched them for a few more minutes then went outside to sit on the wooden chair between the two large ferns on the front lawn. It was a beautiful Saturday morning. The brilliant sunshine was tempered by a nice breeze that carried a hint that rain was on the horizon, perhaps later in the afternoon.

"The police are so corrupt," Maria mused, remembering that high level cop that was on Hernandez's payroll several years ago. That seemed like another lifetime. So much had changed since then. And now the Police Commissioner himself was an accused murderer. And as usual, Terri was at the forefront of the storm. Maria had always been an admirer of hers. And now they were friends, brought together by the man that they had both loved, the father of their sons.

Terri nodded with a half smile. There was nothing she could say in the force's defense. Corruption was a way of life in the police force despite the best efforts of cops like her. But she was determined to make a difference and if the Police Commissioner himself could be brought down, then she was sending a strong message that corruption would not be tolerated – at least not on her watch. It was ironic that the demise of her one time mentor would actually land her the top post much more quickly than she had expected. She had given herself ten years to become the first female Police Commissioner in the western hemisphere. Now it was just a matter of time. The current Deputy Police Commissioner wouldn't last very long at the top post. She would then get the job. No one was more qualified. There would be a lot of grumbling from the old boys' network within the force, and to be frank, some sections of the society, but their bark was worse than their bite. Good sense would prevail and she would be offered the job by the government. And she would take it.

Terri checked the time. It was now 10 a.m. They had been chatting for almost an hour. She was hungry.

"C'mon, let's go have some breakfast," she said to Maria, adding, "I can hear your stomach growling."

Maria laughed heartily. "Yeah right, that was you girl!"

Terri chuckled and they went inside where the boys were still locked in an intense video game battle.

She made them pause it and they all trooped out to the backyard. Mavis, Terri's live in helper, dished out the breakfast of fried Johnny cakes, sausages, Spanish omelet, and French toast sticks that she had prepared, and the foursome dug in hungrily.

The buzzer for the door sounded and Terri got up to answer it when she realized that Mavis was probably in the bathroom as the buzzer kept on ringing.

"Yes?" she queried through the intercom, knowing it must either be one of her neighbours or one of the security guards.

"Ms. Miller?" the voice said.

"Yes?" Terri answered irritably. "Who is it?"

"It's Milton," the man replied. "We have a problem on the complex and need your advice."

"Ok, just a minute," Terri said and quickly made her way to her bedroom to retrieve her firearm. Something wasn't right. Milton had a pronounced lisp that was evident in every syllable he spoke. Whoever it was at the door was not Milton. She slipped an extra clip in the pocket of her shorts and exited the bedroom. Mavis was coming out into the hallway at the same time.

"There might be a problem," Terri whispered. "Lock the kitchen door behind you when you go out to the back yard. Bring the cordless phone with you and call the police if you hear anything."

Mavis nodded, her eyes bulging with fear.

"Go!" Terri urged, giving her a push as it appeared that fear had paralyzed her. Terri then went back out to the front door. Holding the gun down by her right leg, she shifted the curtain slightly to try and see the person's face.

She couldn't.

He was standing directly in front of the door. She looked through the peephole but could only make out the uniform. The person was standing there with his back to the door. She could have told the person to come by the window so that she could see his face but she didn't want to do that and risk him taking flight.

She deactivated the alarm and opened the door.

CHAPTER 29

The man turned around the second Terri opened the door and stepped outside. She gasped. He was very tall – at least 6' 3" with the built of a professional bodybuilder. He looked comical, like a caricature. His legs were spindly like he had completely forgotten about his lower half when he slaved away in the gym. Terri had no idea how they supported his massive bulk.

"You were told to back off the case. You didn't listen. And now you and your family will pay. After I leave here, your parents are next," the man told her matter-of-factly.

Terri trembled at the thought of harm coming to her loved ones. Especially Marc-Anthony. Her knees buckled. He stepped towards her, his massive hands dangling at his sides like a gorilla. Terri raised her gun and fired two quick shots to his torso. He faltered momentarily but to her amazement, kept on coming and treated her to a vicious backhanded slap which propelled her into one of the large ferns on the lawn. He moved with a speed that was surprising for a man of his size. Her head was spinning. She felt like she had been hit with a metal object. She struggled to get up and maintain a grip on her weapon. Smirking as he patted the bullet proof vest that he was wearing underneath the close fitting security guard uniform shirt, he delivered a thunderous kick to her stomach, expelling the small portion of her breakfast that she had managed to consume prior to the meal being disturbed.

The pain was excruciating. She wondered if Mavis had already called the cops and they were on their way. She wondered if no one was witnessing the attack to come to her rescue. She had underestimated the Police Commissioner. Silly her to have thought he would have quietly accepted his fate. The bad guys had finally won. She was going to die. Her only son. His brother. Maria. Mavis. Her parents. No. She couldn't allow it. She was surprised to still feel the gun in her hand. Somehow her fingers were still wrapped around it in a vice grip. He now had one foot on her neck. He was pressing down hard. Cutting off her air supply. She was gasping. Losing consciousness. It was now or never. Ignoring the natural instinct to try and use her hands to pry away his foot, she quickly aimed at his crotch and fired. The man emitted an inhumane scream as his genitals exploded into several pieces.

He fell to the ground with a thud and continued to scream as Terri scrambled to her knees, coughing as she tried to catch her breath. Breathing was so painful that she was sure her ribs were fractured. She collapsed to the ground as she heard the sirens approaching.

The giant was still screaming.

CHAPTER 30

When the police arrived, they were unable to get inside the gated complex. The two security guards were dead, their bodies stuffed inside the small sentry post by the gate. One of them, a senior detective, dialed Terri's home number and told the helper to open the gate. They rushed Terri to the emergency ward of the Caribbean University Hospital where she was immediately examined. Luckily, her ribs were only bruised. Nothing was broken. The right side of her gorgeous face was badly swollen and her neck, which had undergone surgery several years ago when her throat was slashed by the Wolf Man, was also causing her considerable pain. But all in all, she knew that she was lucky. She had cheated death once again. Her attacker was not so lucky. He had died on the way to the hospital. He had lost too much blood. The doctors kept Terri secluded for three hours before allowing her to see anyone.

She then consoled the tearful group of Marc-Anthony, Diego, Mavis, Maria and her parents, who had been anxiously waiting to see her, and after convincing them that she was a little banged up but okay, had a quick meeting with the Deputy Police Commissioner and two senior detectives. The Police Commissioner had set up the hit from jail so he was to be transferred to another jail and only be allowed to speak with his attorney. He was to have access to no one else until it was time for him to go to court.

The Deputy Commissioner also advised Terri that Detective Corporal Jackson had agreed to testify against the Police Commissioner in return for a lesser sentence if the case did indeed go to trial. Terri didn't think that it would. Besides they didn't need Jackson's testimony. He had already confessed to being the triggerman in the shooting death of the lawyer and the knife wielder in the stabbing death of Gilbert Chen. The Police Commissioner himself had strangled the prostitute, Alexandra Fletcher, and ordered the body dumped on the street.

Terri finally got to leave the hospital four and a half hours after her ordeal. The doctor had wanted to keep her overnight for observation but she wasn't having it. After giving her a stern warning to take it easy and telling her to come by for a check up and to change her bandages on Monday, he allowed her to leave.

Terri rode with her parents in their Mercedes sedan while Maria followed in her SUV with Diego and Mavis. Marc-Anthony was snuggled up beside her on the back seat. He had finally stopped crying but his unusual gray eyes were filled with concern for his mother. He didn't know exactly what had happened but it was obvious to him that his mother had been in great danger. He had heard the gunshots and knew that his mother had just gone outside. It had taken every ounce of Mavis' strength to hold him and try to calm him down when they were in the backyard.

The adults did not speak about the incident in front of Marc-Anthony. They quietly listened to Jazz on the radio and when they got to Terri's apartment, her parents left after a few minutes, promising to call her in the morning. Maria left soon after, giving in to Diego's request to spend the night. He did not want to go home. Terri told her it was okay, brushing aside her concern that Diego didn't have any clothes there – Diego and Marc-Anthony both wore the same size – and besides, Marc-Anthony was excited at the prospect of having his brother sleep over.

Terri retired to her room at 10:30 p.m. after tucking in the boys when she finally got them to put aside the videogames and go to bed. She climbed into bed, grimacing at the throbbing pain in her ribs, and called Nico. He was at a video shoot but quickly found a quiet spot at the location so that he could talk. She told him about the incident but downplayed her injuries and the pain. She spoke to him for fifteen minutes and then tried to get some sleep.

Sleep came quickly.

So did bad dreams.

She was fighting the giant again.

This time she lost.

He killed her.

Strangled her to death.

CHAPTER 31

Anna woke up at 7 a.m. on Sunday morning. She had only gotten two hours sleep. She was too excited to close her eyes. Her vacation in hell was almost over. Just a few more hours and her sick, abusive marriage and her psychotic husband would be a terrible memory, instead of her reality. She got up and went to use the bathroom before making her way to the kitchen.

Her husband was already up. He was in the study preparing his sermon for the day. The devil incarnate, leading his flock to the depths of hell. She began to prepare his breakfast, wishing she had the nerve to put some poison in his scrambled eggs. Though she was leaving him, he would simply move on to the next hapless victim. But then again, maybe he would meet his match soon. Maybe the next woman he got married to wouldn't be as docile as she had been. Better to leave him in the hands of the Lord. A wave of shame washed over her and threatened to put a damper on her high spirits when she thought of the degradation and the mental and physical abuse that she had endured at the hands of her husband. She took a deep breath and brushed aside the unpleasant thoughts. No need to dwell on that now when freedom was just hours away. There would be time for reflection later.

She placed his breakfast on a tray and took it to him. She smiled inwardly as she bubbled with happiness. It would be the last time that she would have to prepare him a meal.

Amen to that.

⁂

Erwin Baxter, disgraced Police Commissioner, and former head of the clandestine group known as The Circle, was a shadow of his former authoritative, arrogant self as he sat in his new holding cell. They had transferred him to the compound of the Jamaican Army headquarters the minute he was determined to be the mastermind behind the plot to kill Police Superintendent Terri Miller and her family. He had the dubious distinction of being the first non military personnel to be locked up there. He was to remain there until his court date. He paced the cell slowly, amazed at how quickly and suddenly his life had fallen apart. All because of a dead whore and a cop who fancied herself the saviour of Jamaica. He had been her mentor once, guiding her career and helping her to climb the ranks in unprecedented fashion. And this was the thanks he got. Not once did it occur to her, when she first realized that he was involved, to come to him, tell him what she knew, and offer him a way out. She simply forged ahead and ambushed him. Destroying his life and his career without remorse. He couldn't believe that Tristan "The Giant" Gomez, supposed to be the best at what he did, had failed in his assignment to kill her. The bitch really led a charmed life.

He stopped pacing and looked around the small cell. There was no way he could spend another day in confinement, much less the rest of his life in prison. That was no way to live. At least not for a man like him. He had millions of dollars in the bank but it was about as useful as an extra anus on his elbow. The money could not help him now. He rubbed his nose in agitation. He badly needed a hit. And a piece of rope. He had some cash on him. Twenty thousand dollars. His lawyer had brought it for him as requested. Surely one of the guards wouldn't mind making a quick buck.

Some cocaine and a piece of rope. It would be the last purchase of his life. It was a sobering thought.

Tears filled his eyes and then rolled down the two day stubble on his cheeks.

He wasn't ready to die.

At 9 a.m., Anna and her husband climbed into his Lincoln Navigator and made their way to his small but growing Baptist church, located at the corner of Park and King Streets in the historic section of Riverside, Jacksonville. Competition was stiff, as there were seven churches within a twenty mile radius, including three Baptist churches. They arrived at church, half an hour before the service was to begin, and took their places by the door where they greeted members of the congregation as they filed in. Thirty minutes later, her husband made his way to the pulpit. Sister Alicia, a chartered accountant by profession, choir leader and one of her husband's concubines Anna was sure, led the choir in song to begin the day's service.

Anna's heart pounded as she sang softly in contrast to the boisterous singing being done by the majority of the congregation. It was almost time. The song ended and everyone took their seats. Except Anna. She walked over to the door on the right which led to the restrooms. She didn't look up at the pulpit but she was sure her husband was scowling inwardly.

Probably telling himself that she would pay for being unable to control her bladder during service. Going in the direction of the bathroom was supposed to be a ruse, but she was so nervous and excited that she actually went to the bathroom to pee.

She then walked along the right side of the church, looking straight ahead as she passed the door and windows, sure that people were wondering what she was doing outside but determined not to make eye contact with anyone. She made it around to the front of the church and hopped into a cab that had just let off Mr. Panton, his wife and his mother. She cheerfully told them good morning, ignored their curious stares and told the driver to take her to the Miami International Airport. The driver beamed. He was about to collect a nice fare. It was a long drive to the airport.

She couldn't believe that this was actually happening. She was leaving. As if in disbelief, she looked around out the back window, half expecting to see her husband's black Lincoln Navigator roaring towards them. But it wasn't there. A Dodge Caravan driven by an elderly Caucasian man was the only immediate vehicle behind them.

She noticed that the taxi driver was watching her with a quizzical expression on his broad, heavily bearded face through the rear view mirror. She ignored him and looked out the window.

She was almost free.

Tears rolled down her cheeks.

And for the first time in over a year, she was crying because she was happy.

CHAPTER 32

William Carter, Anna's husband, finished his sermon earlier than he had originally planned. He could not concentrate. Where was his wife? He had not seen her since he glimpsed her walking along the side of the church and that was almost two hours ago. He finished abruptly and after whispering to one of the Deacons to finish the service as he had a serious family emergency, he stepped down from the podium.

He then asked the usher out by the front door if he saw his wife. The young man told him that he saw her go into a cab at the beginning of service and had not seen her return. Carter rushed to his vehicle and hopped in. His head was pounding as he drove out of the church yard speedily, his tyres screeching in protest at the rough handling. He didn't know what kind of stunt she was pulling – maybe the demons that possessed her from time to time had once again taken control. Well he would beat her so badly this evening that they would never return. He broke a few traffic laws and soon pulled up in his driveway. He rushed out of the vehicle and quickly opened the front door and entered the house.

He could sense that she wasn't home. She didn't even have her own house key but he had to check. Where could she have gone? He walked around the house and stroked his goatee, getting angrier by the second. When he found her, and by God he would, she was going to suffer for her sins, just like the good book said she should. He looked inside the closet and her drawers but didn't notice any of her clothing missing. Then a thought struck him and he rushed inside his study and opened the bottom drawer. He hastily threw the contents onto the floor until the drawer was empty. Her passport was missing. He trembled with anger and frustration. Despite the measures he had taken, she had somehow managed to make a run for it. After all he had done for her, she had left him.

He grabbed the phone and took out the directory. He would find out if she was booked on a flight today. He didn't think she would run away from home and stay in the country. She had no friends here. Where else could she go but back to Jamaica? There was no one here to help her so it must have been someone in Jamaica. Maybe that bitch cop had somehow convinced her to leave her marriage and return to Jamaica to live in sin. He leafed through the telephone directory and dialed the number for Jamaica's national airline. Fifteen frustrated minutes later, he dialed the number for America's largest international carrier. Bingo. She had boarded a flight over an hour ago and was on her way to Jamaica.

She was really gone. He couldn't believe that she had the nerve to pull off a stunt like this. He had underestimated her. Shell-shocked, he retrieved the small bottle of Scotch from his top desk drawer and took a long swig. It set his throat on fire but he welcomed the burning sensation. It cleared his mind, allowing him to think of a plan of action. He was going to go and get her and bring her home.

Till death do us part she had sworn on the altar.

And by God that was the way it was going to be.

The only way she could depart his life was by departing this earth.

He called a travel agency to book a flight.

***

Terri went out to the back yard where the two brothers were playing with a soccer ball. She paused at the doorway and watched them momentarily.

177

Everything they did was such a big competition. Marc-Anthony was juggling the ball on his knees while Diego counted and waited his turn impatiently. The ball fell to the ground after 28 juggles. Diego laughed and proclaimed that he could beat that score easily. He did. He juggled up to 32 before the ball touched the ground.

Terri shook her head. They got along great but she was a bit worried about their sibling rivalry. They competed with *everything*. She called them over.

"Would you guys like to go with me to the airport?" she asked, rubbing both their curly manes.

"Yeah!" they answered enthusiastically in unison.

"Ok go get cleaned up," she told them and with that they sprinted inside the house, trying to out run each other.

Thirty minutes later, and against the doctor's orders to relax, Terri and the brothers piled into the SUV that the Mercedes dealer had loaned her until her vehicle was repaired, and made their way to the airport.

"I can't wait to see Auntie Anna!" Marc-Anthony enthused from the back seat.

Terri met his eyes in the rear view mirror.

"Me too honey, me too."

Diego didn't know this 'Auntie Anna' but Marc-Anthony had told him when they were getting dressed that she was pretty so he couldn't wait to see her too.

Terri turned on the massage feature on her seat and as she drove leisurely. She wasn't in any rush.

Anna was due to arrive in forty-five minutes and she would be at the airport in half an hour. She would just get the kids ice cream and wait with them in the VIP lounge at the airport.

Being a celebrity cop did have its perks.

Disgraced Police Commissioner Erwin Baxter was on cloud nine. He had just sniffed two eight balls of cocaine back to back and the euphoric high had allowed him to temporarily soar above his troubles. He was now viewing his sudden and tumultuous fall from grace from a distance, as though it had happened to someone else. God bless the officer on duty. He had done as Baxter as requested, and had gotten him the cocaine and the piece of rope. He had given him the entire twenty thousand dollars though he knew the cocaine and rope wouldn't have cost that much. He wouldn't need it where he was going. The cocaine wasn't of the quality that Baxter was used to but it had done the trick. One final moment of pleasure before he exited this earth. He could now meet his maker with dignity. He decided to proceed quickly, wanting to get it done before the effects of the drug wore off. That would not be good. That would bring him tumbling back to reality. He stood on the small cot and easily tied the rope onto the metallic beam. He was tall, almost as tall as the room, but the three inch difference would be enough.

He methodically made a noose and slipped it around his neck, tightening it.

He then stepped off the cot.

Oh my God, Anna thought as salty tears flowed freely down her sculpted cheeks. *I'm really home.* Though she had been comfortably seated in first class, it was the most uncomfortable plane ride of her life. Not even when her modeling career had been in full flight and she sometimes had to take long trips to places like Hong Kong and Europe, had she been so uncomfortable. Irrationally, she had kept looking over her shoulder, expecting to see her husband, grinning menacingly and asking her if she had really thought she could get away from him.

She was so shaken that the flight attendant, a pretty half-Indian girl with dimples, had asked her on more than one occasion if she was alright. Two glasses of champagne had managed to calm her nerves somewhat. At least she had stopped shaking. She had declined food. It was impossible for her to eat.

She was in a daze looking out the window when she realized with a jolt that it was time to disembark. She exited the plane, ignoring the curious stares of some of the other passengers.

She was still crying.

✶✶✶✶✶✶✶✶✶✶

"Thank you," Terri said, smiling sweetly at the blushing customs officer she had asked to inform her when Anna's flight arrived. It landed five minutes ago. "Anything else Superintendent Miller?" the man asked, happy to assist the popular and surprisingly down to earth police officer.

"Sure, can you have her paged over the intercom to go to the VIP lounge once she has cleared customs?"

"No problem. I'll get on it right away."

"Thanks so much."

The man left and Terri sipped her mocha vanilla latte as she watched the brothers eat their ice cream and argue about who was the best soccer player in the world. Terri smiled and shook her head. Kids nowadays were so different from her generation. They were exposed to so much more at an early age. She could only imagine what the world would be like by the time they grew up and had kids of their own. She smiled at the thought of being a grandmother. Thankfully that was at least fifteen years away.

She could hear Anna being paged on the PA system. She was excited. She hadn't seen her best friend in so long.

She could see the entrance to the VIP lounge from where she was sitting and three minutes later, Anna entered the lounge with a nervous, teary smile. Terri got up and ran over to her, hugging her tightly. Anna sobbed uncontrollably; overwhelmed by being home and away from the beast she had mistakenly married. Terri hushed her soothingly, not in the least embarrassed by the curious stares they were getting from the other people in the VIP lounge. Terri gestured to the kids to come over and they all trooped out to the parking lot. Anna's tears subsided enough for her to greet the kids properly by the time they got to the vehicle.

"Why are you crying Auntie Anna?" Marc-Anthony asked, his intense grey eyes brimming with concern. He loved his auntie. She was very nice and always gave him a lot of cool gifts.

"Because I'm happy honey," Anna replied. She kissed him and then kissed Diego and ruffled his hair.

Terri squeezed her hand reassuringly as they headed out.

She couldn't wait to get home and find out what had happened to Anna.

CHAPTER 33

"So...let me get this straight. You two were the last soldiers on duty but neither of you happen to know how the Police Commissioner had gotten cocaine and rope in his cell?" Major Graham asked incredulously. The dead body of the Police Commissioner had just been discovered and the Major was hopping mad. Two tiny empty bags had been on the ground in the cell and it was obvious that they had contained cocaine.

The two privates remained silent. There was no way the guilty one was going to confess and there was no way the other one would snitch on him. The athletic Private Sangster was a popular figure around the base as he captained both the cricket and the soccer teams which always did well in their respective competitions. If he snitched on him he would be treated as a pariah around the base. He would have to suck up whatever punishment was coming though he didn't do anything.

The Major glared at the two men before him. One of them had caused him a public relations nightmare. The army would look very bad if the circumstances surrounding the Police Commissioner's death became public. Obviously one of the guards had been bribed to procure the items for the Commissioner. He suspected it was Sangster but he couldn't prove it. He would have to liaise with the coroner and cover it up. He sighed angrily. He didn't need this shit. He had enough to worry about.

"Get out of my sight and confine yourselves to your barracks until I decide what to do about you fucking imbeciles," he seethed.

"Sir, yes sir!" the privates said in unison and quickly exited the office.

The Major picked up the phone and called the coroner.

✵✶✷✸✹✺✻

"Are you ok...you left very suddenly today," Sister Alicia probed as she spoke to William. She knew that whatever was going on had something to do with his wife. She left church and had not returned.

William sighed. He was half drunk and seething with anger and frustration.

"She left me," he replied, draining his second glass of brandy. He had already polished off the small bottle of scotch and had moved on to brandy on the rocks.

"My goodness!" Sister Alicia exclaimed, trying to mask her pleasure at the news. "What a wicked woman! I cannot believe that she would do that to you."

"I'm going for her and bring her back," he continued, staring at the painting of him and his wife on the wall. It had been done by a young man from the congregation who was a talented artist.

No! Sister Alicia screamed inwardly. She could not allow that to happen. Not when she was so close to having the pastor all to herself. She was a member of his church for eight months and she had been having an affair with him since a week after she joined. She loved him. And she deserved to have him. Not that washed up supermodel who couldn't even cook her husband a decent meal. She wasn't even spiritually in tune with him. Good riddance.

"You don't sound too good William," she said. "I'm going to come over and take care of you. You need me right now."

William was still staring at the painting. Anna was such a beautiful woman. Not even the demons that regularly possessed her could change her exotic beauty. He had to get her back.

"Okay," he responded morosely. At least she could help release some of the anger and frustration that currently had him in a prison-like vise. His flight was tomorrow morning. He would get a hotel room in Kingston and visit the cop. She wouldn't be hard to find. And once he found her, he would find Anna.

Sister Alicia quickly hung up and hurried home. She was going to change out of her church clothes and slip into something more comfortable. Hopefully she would be able to spend the night. Finally being able to sleep with William in his matrimonial bed would be pure bliss.

❋❋❋❋❋❋❋

Anna played with the kids for awhile and then they all had an early dinner out by the patio. Mavis had cooked oxtail and beans, baked chicken, rice and peas, macaroni and cheese, fried plantain and potato salad. Anna was in heaven. It was the first meal she was having since she got married to William that she hadn't prepared herself. He had never taken her out to eat, not even once. After dinner, while the kids amused themselves with video games, Terri and Anna retreated to Terri's bedroom with a bottle of white wine. Terri then listened in horror as Anna, in between emotional breakdowns, told her in graphic detail everything that she had been through in the past year.

Sister Alicia smiled as she removed William's dick from her mouth and rolled on the condom which she had taken out of her bag. The expiry date had long passed and the condom would break with the slightest friction. She was counting on it.

She wanted him to get her pregnant. With his seed in her belly, he would forget about that Jamaican witch and marry her, the mother of his child. Or risk a terrible scandal that would destroy the church that he had worked so hard to build. She was positive that he would choose the former.

He groaned as she lowered herself onto his rigid shaft. She rode him hard and fast, smiling when she heard the sound that she was waiting for. The condom had popped. She lowered her head and sucked his right nipple as she bounced slowly, clenching her pelvic muscles. The result was predictable. He moaned loudly and started thrusting wildly upwards as he climaxed.

She held him tight as he trembled from the after-shocks of his orgasm. Pleased with herself, she removed the torn condom and went into the bathroom to dispose of it. He had fallen asleep by the time she returned. She rubbed her stomach lovingly as she stood watching him, as though she could already feel the baby. She recited a silent prayer as she watched his sleeping form.

She just *had* to have his baby.

It was the key to becoming Mrs. William Carter.

And she wanted to be his wife more than anything else in this world.

CHAPTER 34

Anna woke up at 9 a.m. on Monday morning. She stayed in bed for awhile, looking out the window at the beautiful scenery and savouring her first morning as a liberated woman. She was back home, back in the company of the people who loved her and eventually, with their love and support, would manage to overcome the horrors she had been through at the hands of her husband. As soon as she got settled, she would seek the advice of a good attorney and get a divorce. That would be the first step on the road to some level of normalcy. She spoke with Terri for hours last night, and it had helped tremendously, being able to share her pain with someone who knew her inside out and would just listen and be compassionate without judging her. She took a quick shower and went out to the living room. Mavis was doing some light tidying up and smiled broadly when she saw her.

"Good morning Ms. Anna," she said. "Ready for some breakfast?"

"Good morning Mavis. Yes, thanks. I'll have it out on the patio," Anna told her.

She was soon digging into thin, delectable salt fish fritters along with bacon, scrambled eggs and toast.

Terri had told her to just relax for a few days and don't worry about anything just yet.

She would do just that.

⁂

Terri looked at the group of nine before her. Eight men and one woman. Some of the most powerful and wealthy people in the island. The Circle. Minus its now dead founder and enforcer, Police Commissioner Erwin Baxter. Terri had been shocked and disappointed to hear that he had died of a heart attack last night. Death was too easy. She had wanted him to go to prison for a very long time.

She was supposed to be home recuperating but she had ordered them to meet with her this morning and did not want to cancel.

"I can only imagine some of the illegal activities that you people have been engaged in," she began without preamble, her eyes scanning the group as she spoke. They were all seated in three rows of three. "Luckily for you, the only concrete evidence I have so far on the activities of your clandestine group pointed to Erwin Baxter and his ECU thugs. But I have no doubt, that there is more dirt out there, waiting to be discovered."

She sipped from her bottled water and looked pointedly at Elizabeth Martin-Cole, the Attorney General, and continued.

"Some of you hold important public offices, and have been using your positions for personal gain. I urge you to desist. I urge you to disband. I have an open file on you people and I will be watching. And God help you if we cross paths again for the wrong reason. Good day, lady and gentlemen."

They looked at each other as if to say *I can't believe this bitch made us come down here to give us a fucking lecture.*

They filed out of her office quickly and soon she was alone.

She had seen the smirk on Elizabeth Martin-Cole's face. She knew that they would continue to live as though they were above the law and she knew that they were quite upset at being summoned to her office like truant school children. She also knew that they were very powerful enemies to have. But she didn't care. She had power too, and God and the law were on her side. She buzzed her secretary to get someone to remove the extra chairs from her office. Her ribs were aching. She was ready to go back home.

The Circle met at the poolside of Elizabeth Martin-Cole's palatial spread in Beverly Hills immediately after leaving Police Headquarters. They laughed and mocked Terri Miller before they got down to business. They were not scared of her. She was a formidable opponent but she could be handled. Besides, she had only become aware of their existence because of Baxter's stupidity. Those days were over, things would be different now.

The motion was put forward and all were in agreement that they would move forward with Martin-Cole as their leader. They would meet for the weekend at an exclusive resort in Negril where they would plan the road ahead. Half an hour later, they all went their respective ways.

❧❧❧❧❧❧❧

William Carter slipped on his sunglasses as he got ready to exit the plane. He had only his carry-on, as he didn't plan to be in Jamaica for longer than three days. He made his way to customs and twenty minutes later, he was outside in the brilliant sunshine.

He procured the services of one of the three men who asked him if he wanted a taxi, and was soon on his way to New Kingston where he planned to book into one of the hotels. He told the taxi man of his plans and the man advised him to try out the French

Court Hotel which had recently been renovated and was now the most popular destination for business travelers staying in Kingston. They got there in forty minutes and luckily, he was able to get a room due to the fact that a contingent of Chinese businessmen had just checked out.

The taxi man waited while he checked in and then took him over to Police Headquarters.

"Do you know Terri Miller?" he asked the taxi driver, who had introduced himself as Bumpy, while they waited for the light to change on Knutsford Boulevard.

"De police woman? Yeah man! Trust me...she come in like a national hero. De people love her bad," he related enthusiastically, scratching one of the many pimples on his face as he spoke. "Ah yuh friend?"

"No," he responded curtly and that was the end of the conversation.

They arrived at Police Headquarters and he instructed Bumpy to wait for him in the parking lot. He strode purposefully into the building and stopped at the front desk.

A uniformed female officer looked at him questioningly.

When he realized that she wasn't about to ask him nicely if she could help him, he told her that he was here to see Terri Miller.

She wordlessly picked up the phone and dialed an extension.

So damn rude, he mused in annoyance while he waited.

"She's not in office," the woman told him when she got off the phone.

"Well, is she expected to return for the day?" Carter asked. "It's very important that I speak with her. I've come all the way from Florida just to meet with her."

Apparently the cop was not impressed.

Rolling her eyes, she told him that she was not privy to the Superintendent's itinerary and had no idea if she would be back for the day.

Carter stormed out without uttering another word.

What now?

Bumpy spotted him and exited the parking lot, stopping at his feet. He got in and slammed the door.

"Go easy man," Bumpy chided. He was very protective of his car and particularly hated when his door was slammed. "Where to now?"

Carter didn't respond immediately.

"I don't know," he finally replied. "I need to see Terri Miller but she's not there and I need to find her urgently."

Bumpy smiled.

"Mi know where she live...ah nuh big secret which part she live but de t'ing is yuh can't just go dere and see her just so...yuh haffi 'ave appointment fi get inna de complex. Strong security over deh...a pure big shot live inna de complex."

Carter's face brightened considerably. This man was a Godsend.

"Let me worry about that. Just take me there."

Bumpy did his bidding, happily doing his calculations as he drove. He was going to earn a lot of money from his grumpy American passenger today.

Terri was reminiscing about old times with Anna on the patio when she heard the intercom.

"I'll get it!" she shouted to Mavis.

She used the one by the front door.

"Yes?"

She listened momentarily.

"Send him in," she instructed.

"I'll be right back," she told Anna and went outside, closing the door behind her.

CHAPTER 35

The heavy-set armed guard opened the gate and Bumpy drove into the complex. He was impressed.

"Yuh ah big shot man," he said as he noticed Terri Miller standing in front of one of the apartments.

Carter didn't respond. He saw her too. He was suddenly nervous though he didn't know why. It was almost as though she was expecting him.

Bumpy pulled up and excitedly said hi to Terri.

She politely responded with a smile. Carter exited the cab and went over to her.

She looked at him for several seconds and the hatred he saw in her eyes made him look away.

"Follow me," she said curtly.

He walked behind her and joined her on an antique looking bench underneath a tree that he didn't recognize.

"Look I'm —"

Terri gave him the hand.

"Just shut up and listen," she told him.

His mouth tightened and his eyes blazed in anger but he remained silent.

"I was informed the minute you arrived in the island. There is an all point bulletins issued for you. I know where you are staying. I know everything. People are awaiting my instructions as we speak. If you do as I say, you will be allowed to leave with no problems. Refuse and your life will be a living hell."

Carter didn't speak for a while. After the shock of the things she had said wore off, he went on the offensive.

"I'm not a criminal. Why would there be an all points bulletin out for me? This is illegal. I can sue the police force and the stupid hotel for invasion of privacy among other things. I simply came here to get my wife and I'm not leaving without her."

Terri stood up and looked down at him like he was the dirtiest, most disgusting thing that she had ever laid eyes upon.

"You're worse than a criminal. You maggot. You don't deserve the air you breathe...you monster. I should kill you but luckily for you, I'm not a cold blooded killer. But I love my friend and I will do *anything* to protect her. This is what is going to happen if you don't go back to the hotel now and sign the divorce papers that my lawyer has drawn up. I am going to make a call, and acting on a tip, of course, two detectives will find twenty ounces of cocaine in your bag, as well as two pounds of compressed marijuana. You will be arrested and charged, and thrown into jail where you will be raped and beaten long before you are able to get legal representation. And when you do, you will be denied bail because of your flight risk. Your case will be put off over and over again. Who knows, you might even die before you get sentenced. Your choice ass-hole. You've got five seconds before I make that call."

Carter shivered like he was cold. He felt weak and nauseated. He couldn't believe what he was hearing. Was she really that powerful? And cruel? It wasn't in his best interest to call her bluff. His life was at stake.

"Ok, I'll do it," he croaked.

Terri did make a call but it was to her lawyer.

"He's on his way," was all she said and then hung up.

"When you get back to the hotel, look around the lobby for a dark, bearded man wearing a blue pinstripe suit. Once you have signed the papers, call the airline and get your flight moved up. If you are still in the island by midday tomorrow, everything I described will still occur. Now get the fuck out of here."

Seemingly paralyzed by shock, he didn't move imme-diately. Terri slapped his face. Hard. So hard her injured ribs groaned in protest. She ignored them and slapped him again.

"I said get the fuck out of here," she hissed.

He moved quickly now, and was soon in the back of the cab. Bumpy, his eyes still wide from what he just witnessed, headed out, glancing in the rearview at his passenger every chance he got.

He appeared close to tears.

Bumpy tried hard to suppress a chuckle.

CHAPTER 36

Later that night, William Carter was in his hotel room nursing a bottle of potent Jamaican rum which he chased with a grapefruit tinged soft drink. He easily spotted the lawyer in the lobby when he returned from his horrible meeting with Terri Miller, and had signed the papers without a word. He had then called the airline and the earliest flight he could get on was for tomorrow morning at 6:20. He couldn't wait to leave this place. Damn third world death trap. After paying Bumpy for his services, and asking him to pick him up at 4 a.m. to take him to the airport, he had dined alone in the hotel restaurant, watching dazedly as exuberant travelers chatted jovially and indulged their palettes with exotic Jamaican dishes. Their happiness made him nauseous.

He had purchased the rum and soft drink and retired to his room after dinner. He was there, wallowing in a bottomless abyss of self pity, drinking and watching T.V. though he could not concentrate. He continued to surf aimlessly, stopping when he got to a porn channel. There was a tall, exotic looking woman pleasuring herself with a ribbed pink dildo. She reminded him of Anna. He turned off the T.V. in anguish and threw the remote control on the floor. He would never see her again. All because of that wicked, meddling cop.

He damned her soul to hell.

⁂

The following day, Terri went to see her doctor and he gave her a check-up, changed her bandages and severely reprimanded her for not obeying his orders. After promising to take the rest of the week off, she went home and was pleased to see that the lawyer had dropped off Anna's divorce papers. Anna had just gotten out of bed when she returned home so they had a late breakfast out on the patio.

Terri slid the manila envelope across the table.

"What's this?" Anna queried, wiping her hands on a napkin before reaching for the envelope.

Terri merely smiled and chewed on her muffin.

Anna opened the envelope and tears ran down her cheeks as she read the contents. She got up and rushed over to Terri. She hugged her so tightly that Terri had difficulty breathing.

"How...oh my God...I can't..." Anna mumbled, so overcome with emotion that she was unable to articulate her thoughts.

Terri told her what had gone down with Carter. Anna shook her head in disbelief. Only Terri could have pulled that off. She didn't know what she would do without her. She got a pen and attached her signature to the documents. Terri then called a bearer to take them back to the lawyer's office.

Anna was now a free woman.

CHAPTER 37

Terri decided that her injuries not withstanding, now was as good a time as any for Nico to come and visit her. Anna was doing much better, she was off from work for the rest of the week including the weekend, and she missed him terribly. Nico was ecstatic when he received her call. He immediately booked a flight and would be in Jamaica at 7 a.m. Tuesday morning. Terri was so excited that she was finding it difficult to sleep.

She had prepared Marc-Anthony for Nico's visit by telling him that a special friend was coming to visit her and she hoped that he would like him. Marc-Anthony had looked at her in surprise before cheekily asking if the guy was her boyfriend. Terri had laughed and sheepishly told him yes. Her son found it hilarious that his mother had a boyfriend. Terri was a bit surprised at his reaction but at least he wasn't exhibiting any signs of jealousy. Not yet anyway.

His grandfather aside, he didn't have a father figure in his life so she had expected him to be apprehensive about another man being in their lives. When Marc-Anthony was three years old, he had asked her about his father and she told him that he had passed away in a tragic accident before he was born. He sometimes asked her details about his father from time to time but hadn't mentioned him in over a year. She was so happy that he and his brother got along well. She hoped that would continue to be the case as they got older.

She looked over at Anna who was fast asleep on the right side of her bed. Anna was looking forward to meeting Nico as well. She had offered to leave the house so that Terri could have her privacy but Terri had told her that it was ok as Nico would be staying at a hotel. She didn't think it was appropriate to have him staying there on his first visit. Terri's parents owned an apartment at a complex on Lady Musgrave drive and had given the tenant notice so that Anna could stay there. Terri didn't want Anna to go any-where until the apartment was ready and that would-n't be for another month. She was happy to have her best friend staying with her. It was just like old times.

Quite some time passed before Terri eventually fell asleep.

Nico slipped on his oversized Gucci aviators and stepped out into the early morning sunshine. Jamaica. It was his first visit but it wouldn't be his last. Who knows, depending on how things progressed with Terri, it just might become his home. It would be a big adjustment as he had never lived outside of New York, and he had his business to run, but he would do anything to be with her. He loved her that much. He pretended not to notice the flirtatious smile of the voluptuous girl in the close fitting red and grey Juicy Couture sweat suit, and looked straight ahead as he made his way to customs. She had sat a couple of seats away from him in first class and according to tidbits of her conversation with the guy seated next to her that he couldn't help but overhear as she had spoken so loudly, she was a Jamaican singer who was returning from doing a few shows in New York and Connecticut. He collected his suitcase and while in the line to go through customs, one of the officers came up to him.

"Mr. Sanchez?" the man queried.

"Yes..." Nico responded guardedly.

"Come with me please," the man instructed politely though it was clear that he wasn't asking.

Nico wondered what the hell was going on. He remained calm however; confident that one phone call to Terri would solve any problem that he might encounter. She should be outside to pick him now anyway.

The stern faced customs officer led him to a small windowless room and told him to sit. The man then left, locking the door behind him.

Nico took out his mobile and turned it on. He didn't like the looks of this at all. Obviously this was an interrogation room of sorts. He needed to get through to Terri. His first visit to Jamaica was off to a rocky start. Just as his phone picked up the signal for one of the local cell phone providers, the door burst open suddenly, startling him.

Terri entered the room wearing a mischievous smile.

"You're under arrest, Nico Sanchez," she purred, locking the door behind her and climbing on top of his lap. "For breaching the dangerously sexy looks act."

Nico grinned, both with relief and pleasure.

"What's my sentence?" he asked, playing along.

"Life with me...hard labour," she breathed, before claiming his lips in a passionate kiss.

She broke the kiss and got up when she felt his dick straining against his jeans. Terri had surprised herself with her actions. She had planned to be very low key when Nico arrived as she didn't want the press to get wind of her budding romance but here she was, throwing caution to the wind. She didn't give a shit who knew. She was in love and had no problem showing it.

"You devil...you got me big time...I owe you one," Nico said in a strained voice as Terri led him outside. God he had missed her. Terri was one of a kind. So beautiful and sophisticated, yet spontaneous and loving.

She waved her thanks to the customs officer who had assisted her with the prank while Nico grinned sheepishly as they walked by. They walked hand in hand to the parking lot and climbed into her SUV.

Nico kissed her again as soon as they got inside the vehicle.

Terri moaned in his mouth. She was so wet her underwear felt uncomfortable.

"Mmmm...I'm so happy that you're here baby," she sighed contentedly and started the engine.

She couldn't wait to get to the hotel to show Nico just how badly she missed him.

CHAPTER 38

Nico's eyes rolled to the back of his head as he navigated the turbulent waters of Terri's sea of love and lust, the strong intense waves rocking his core over and again, driving him blissfully crazy.

He felt deranged, like he didn't have control of his faculties.

He was delirious, like a first time heroin user.

"I love you...I love you...I love you..." Nico whispered over and over and again as he gripped her tightly and expelled his children inside her. She wrapped her legs around him, welcoming his seed and joining him in his orgasmic coma.

She had climaxed twice already, but this last simultaneous orgasm was so intense that she literally felt a pain in her heart.

They stayed in each other's arms, shuddering, for what seemed like an eternity.

Nico finally pulled out of her and gently extricated himself from her embrace. He looked at her. Her gorgeous face was sporting an indescribable expression. He got up from off the bed and walked unsteadily over to his luggage.

Terri propped herself up on her elbows.

"What are you doing hun? Come back to bed..." she protested, wanting to cuddle.

He didn't respond but kept rummaging through the bag until he found what he was looking for.

He rose and came over to the bed, holding a small box in his hand.

"Come here," he commanded hoarsely.

Terri got up slowly, her eyes darting from the box in his hand to the intense look on his face. She swung her toned legs onto the carpeted floor and stood in front him.

He sank to one knee, his face close enough to her shaven essence for his breath to tickle her clit. He looked up at her as he removed the ring from the box and held her left hand.

Terri's heart did an acrobatic somersault.

"I've loved you since the day we met. And I know I'll love you for as long as I live. You are without a doubt my soul mate Terri...will you marry me?"

"Yes...yes Nico...I'll be your wife..." she responded in a cracked voice. Tears flowed freely down her face.

Nico slipped the ring on and she crumbled to the floor on top of him. She found his lips and devoured them hungrily. Soon he was inside her again, rigid and powerful, and she rode him like a woman possessed, rode his dick like she owned it.

When he ejaculated, she felt it in her soul.

Anthony no longer owned her heart.

Nico had claimed it.

The realization intensified her orgasm.

EPILOGUE

Erwin Baxter was buried two weeks after his suicide. He was not given a State funeral befitting someone of his status due to the severity of the crimes he had committed. Only his family, close friends, loyal cops who had benefited financially and otherwise by engaging in criminal activities on his behalf, and members of the media attended.

Baxter's main enforcer, Detective Corporal Jackson, and six other members of the Elite Crimes Unit, were in jail where they were being held without bail pending their sentencing. None of them would receive less than ten years.

Detective Corporal Foster was still on sick leave. His jaw had been broken in two places and he would be away from work for at least ninety days.

The Circle, now with eight members, and with Elizabeth Martin-Cole as their leader, forged ahead. Things were different now; no more code names and no one person would be allowed to make decisions that affected the entire group in isolation. They would operate like a conglomerate with Martin-Cole as their CEO. With an unquenchable thirst for wealth and power, their aim was to collectively be worth more than the GDP of Jamaica by 2020.

William Carter, Anna's ex-husband, killed himself two days after his brief visit to Jamaica. In a fit of rage over too much salt being in his dinner, he had choked Sister Alicia to death in the kitchen and then realizing what he had done, and hearing the sirens approaching the house after one of his neighbours had dialed 911, he had rushed to the study and retrieved his firearm. The cops heard the single shot as they attempted to enter the house. They later found him slumped in the chair behind his desk with a hole in his head.

His eyes were open.

Everybody loved Nico. Terri's parents, Anna, Mavis, and most importantly, Marc-Anthony. It was like he had always been part of the family. Everyone, especially her parents, were surprised at the engagement but wisely didn't make a big deal out of Terri keeping Nico a secret from them. Terri was certain she had conceived on the day Nico proposed, and said as much to him. They would know for sure in another month but as far as Terri was concerned, she was positive that she had a little girl in her stomach. They decided to get married quickly, whether she was pregnant or not. Terri and her mom immediately began making wedding plans. They would get married on the beach at a five star resort in Portland.

For the first time in her life, Terri felt as though she had all the pieces together. She was almost at the pinnacle of her illustrious career, she had the best son a mother could ask for, and soon, in another eight weeks, she would be a married woman.

She looked up at the stars from her perch on the patio and thanked God for all her blessings.

CPSIA information can be obtained at www.ICGtesting.com
Printed in the USA
BVOW021154120412

287517BV00001B/8/P